For Frank and Rene -
Thanks for the D.N.A.

Thank you to my proof-readers:
Bryan Cutler and Elizabeth Luff

Thank you to the designer: Karen Creed, Ignite Creative

Published by Lamplight Productions
Samples of Mark Clark's other
writings and songs can be found at:
**www.markclark.com.au**

# PROLOGUE

# CORPORATE CITY – 2171

EXT.PRESIDENT'S PENTHOUSE.DAY

Clouds swirl around the top of a skyscraper.

Through the shifting cloud, people can be seen moving inside.

INT.PRESIDENT'S PENTHOUSE.DAY

Several adults talk and laugh at a social gathering.

A LITTLE GIRL of about ten and a LITTLE BOY of about six play together on the floor.

A YOUNG MAN in his late teens watches them play.

The little girl chases after a runaway ball. It lands at the young man's feet.

> YOUNG MAN
> Those are pretty ribbons you have in your hair.

The little girl smiles sweetly.

The young man stares at her as he hands the ball back.

# CORPORATE CITY – 2191

The city looms upon the horizon. The afternoon sun is

setting in the west. The buildings are punctuated by its golden, dying rays. Clouds hang pendulously above the city. Centrepoint Tower can be seen intermittently through the drifting low-level cloud.

In the foreground sits the wasteland.

ANGLE ON to the head of Centrepoint Tower.

DISSOLVE

INT.CENTREPOINT TOWER.DAY

The room is alive with elegantly dressed women and men in suits. They are served canapés by white-suited waiters.

There are perhaps fifty guests. Among them is ELIZABETH DAWSON, a particularly attractive woman of about thirty. She is stately, impeccably dressed, olive-skinned, has long, swirling dark hair and piercing blue-green eyes. She is admiring the view and is herself being admired by a host of men who appear overly attentive to her every word.

Aside, stands DAMIEN HILL. He is in his mid-twenties. He is tall, lean, handsome and relaxed in his movements like a man who takes no nonsense and is handy in a stoush. His hair is short and blond. His features are strong and rugged. He is not conventionally handsome but he is striking. He possesses an easy-going Australian country charm. He has a peculiar animal magnetism. A group of women flutter about him.

Surreptitiously, he looks in Elizabeth's direction.

She too, though thronged by admirers, has noticed him.

She pulls a WAITER aside. She motions towards Damien.

> ELIZABETH
> Who is that young man?

> WAITER
> That is Damien Hill, miss, of Hill Enterprises.

> ELIZABETH
> Give him this.

She hands the waiter a business card. He nods and leaves.

She is about to return to her group of admirers when a man in his late twenties approaches her.

This is LESLIE WOODFORD. He is fair-skinned and plain featured. His eyes are large and brown like a puppy dog's and he is losing his hair prematurely. He is modestly dressed and his clothes hang off him, hinting at his skinny body beneath.

> LESLIE
> Excuse me, President Dawson?

She waits.

LESLIE
My name is Leslie Woodford. I'm one of your
consuls for the next six years.

He shakes her hand.

The other men gathered around her look
condescendingly at him.

LESLIE
It's wonderful to meet you.

ELIZABETH
Thank you.

Leslie hesitates, aware of the eyes trained upon him.

LESLIE
I'm looking forward to working with you and
Consul Brand. I already have some ideas,
some scientific notions and inventions . . .

One of the young men interrupts rudely.

YOUNG MAN
Elizabeth, finish your story.

The other young men take up the chorus.

ELIZABETH
We'll talk later, consul.

She turns back to her admirers.

Leslie smiles, nods obsequiously and moves away.

He notices a young man who has just turned from the bar. Leslie approaches him.

This is NICHOLAS BRAND. He is in his forties. He is well-dressed, slightly overweight, relatively short, and has a rounded and affable face. When he smiles his eyes almost disappear into the creases surrounding them.

LESLIE
Excuse me, Mister Brand, I'm . . .

NICHOLAS
Leslie   Woodford.  Congratulations  on  your appointment. Call me Nick.

The men smile and shake hands.

ANGLE ON to Damien in the foreground. The waiter has just handed him Elizabeth's card. He looks over the lip of his champagne glass towards Elizabeth, who has caught eyes with him but just as suddenly turns away, flicks back her great, dark hair and laughs at some clever comment with her bright, white teeth gleaming mischievously. Men are swarmed around her like locusts to honey.

Her laughter amplifies in reverb and tumbles away. The camera flows with its recession down the long, thin shaft of the tower and shatters into the streets below.

EXT.CITY STREET.AFTERNOON

A woman and small child suckling from her breast sit in

the shadow of the tower. The woman is dressed in rags. A cold wind whips around her. She pulls her child in closer.

Beside her, her husband stands upon a soap box. He is red headed, bearded and bedraggled. His teeth are rotted, he is unwashed and his hair is a matted mess. He is cold but he speaks passionately.

A group of similarly bedraggled spectators have gathered and are listening to him, in spite of the cold spits of rain which have begun to fall upon them.

MAN ON SOAP BOX

So while we work and suffer deprivation, the rich live above us in their skyscrapers. They never have to work. They never have to suffer. But look at us. We've got no power.
> (points to the tower above)

They call this a democracy? Rubbish! Rubbish, I say! Two new consuls have been appointed this very day. Where do they come from? The scrapers. Who do they really represent?
> (waving an admonishing finger towards the crowd)

Not us down here, fellow Corporate City-Siders. Not us.

A voice is thrown up from the crowd.

VOICE

One of the two is a thinker. He'll fight for us.

MAN ON SOAP BOX

Don't be so naïve. The rich let one of the smart ones get elected every so often to keep us quiet. Look at the facts – there's only been two in the last sixty years and what did they achieve for us? Nothing. The rest are all scraper dwellers. You'll see comrades, he'll fall into line just like the others. Look around you. Does this look like a fair world to you?

The man sweeps his arm along the line of the city street. The camera pans with it.

Everywhere is filth and deprivation. Women hunt for food among the gutters. Scraps fly, enraged by the wind. Old men forage in bins for cigarette butts. Others stuff paper into metal bins. They make fires to ward off the growing winter chill.

Large guards stand menacingly outside of opulent skyscrapers, shooing children swathed in rags away from the foyers.

One guard steps back under the cover of the building. It begins to rain in earnest.

# Chapter 1

It was late June. Yet again the heavens had opened. It had rained hard on and off for several weeks now and the weather had been unusually cold. The homeless had been carted away by the truckful. The morgue in Kent Street was busier than usual and the ovens in Lilyfield had been spewing them out to God twenty-four hours a day. Not even the incessant rain could dampen that fire.

Under the latest downpour, Elizabeth, Leslie and Nicholas were herded under umbrellas through the large iron gates of the Oxford Street Barracks and into a large, bare room. A corporal took their coats and a sergeant ushered them into a smaller, more comfortable office further inside the building. Here, a lieutenant welcomed them, showed them through to the seats within, and withdrew.

The three sat silently for a short while, shaking off imaginary water and settling into their red leather lounge chairs. Leslie stole several furtive glances at Elizabeth but she seemed self-contained and unreceptive to his silent solicitations. She was incredibly stylish and beautiful, he was thinking. Her full-length dress was black and fringed with white around collar and hem. Her olive skin was soft and flawless and above her breasts was visible an ellipse of pearls, settled comfortably beneath her slender neck.

Leslie cast a glance towards Nicholas, to see whether he had noticed his silent appreciation of Elizabeth. If he had, Nicholas showed no signs of it. He sat passively. Leslie watched him for a moment more. He was short, soft and likeably rotund, rather than hard and stumpy looking. In fact, he cut a stylish figure in his well-cut suit and tie. His face was endearing and welcoming. His eyes were brown and doleful, like a sad child's. But right now he looked self-satisfied, as a man might well be, having just been elected to high office.

Leslie looked down at his clothes and was suddenly aware of his own poverty. He dismissed the thought at once. These were details an inventor need not dwell upon, he assured himself. Vanity is not an attribute worthy of a good mind.

The three had not long to wait before the door opened and into the room stepped a tall, thin man of middle years. He wore the epaulettes of a two-star general and carried a little rider's crop.

'Sorry I'm late,' he apologised, shaking everybody's hand. 'Damn rain.'

He offered no further apology and no-one cared to have him qualify. All three were anxious to begin the briefing.

'Well, here we are,' the general continued, coughing prior to beginning his oration. He nodded to some unseen presence in the wall behind.

Leslie looked back in time to see a thumbs-up return from an embrasure carved in the rear wall of the room. Presently the lights dimmed and the general, rather theatrically, stepped into the light of the projector before any image was projected. As he spoke, a screen slid into place behind him.

'Congratulations Consuls Brand and Woodford on your election to six-year office. Your election is a great honour and with it comes considerable responsibility. Welcome back also, President Dawson, for your second term at the helm of Corporate City. I don't need to tell you all that the information to which you will now be privy must never be divulged to those outside of office, even after your term is completed. You've already sworn an oath to this effect, but I remind you of it now before you see the following presentation.'

He nodded again to the projectionist and withdrew to one side.

Elizabeth, Nicholas and Leslie sat, bathed by the flickering glow. Leslie sneaked one last brief glance towards Elizabeth. She had a slight upturning of her lips. Had she noticed him? He nestled back into his seat as the presentation began.

Revealed upon the screen was an elderly man. He appeared to be somewhere in his eighties. He had little wisps of grey hair about his temples and wore glasses that amplified the brightness of his dark eyes. His neck was flaccid like a tortoise's, the skin weighed down by gravity and by the passage of the years. His face had a boyish, soft appearance. His cheeks, for all the years that were etched upon them, were still rubicund and lustrous. His voice was educated and English, and though it had shrivelled with time to a soft, ghostly shadow of its former self, it was still passionate but considered. It was still the voice of Sir Colin Dunnett.

'The year is 2096,' he began. I leave this recording to those who would govern this city in future years. It has been nearly twenty-two years since the establishment of the new government. Under the presidency of Jeremiah we have had our triumphs and our problems, but the details of this you can read for yourselves in the briefs I have organised for each of you. Suffice to say that it is the wish of the current administration that a triumvirate is to be formed every six years to govern this city and that it should be made up of three persons from diverse social background elected by every adult member of the city's population. Two consuls are to be elected every six years to support a president, who shall preside for twelve.

We have now a city of approximately two hundred and seventy thousand people, the majority of whom are relatively poor. We have not, as yet been able to till the land beyond the outskirts of the city, but hopefully, whenever it is in the future that you are listening, this frustrating abnormality of the wasteland soil will have been overcome. Unfortunately, at this time, we can only grow within the city itself and its immediate surrounds. Due to this we cannot, as yet provide for a growing population. We have therefore, regrettably, been forced to enforce a population cap of two children per couple in an attempt to stabilise population size. With time, this too may change.

It is envisioned that every so often a recording of this type will be made as a basic guide as to the wishes of your forefathers. It is hoped that putting a human face and voice to our ideals will help guide you through the no doubt torrid years ahead. Perhaps these short snippets will remind you of why we do what we do and remind you that we govern not for our own self-interest, but for the good of all citizens. Remember, consuls, that man is somewhere between ape and angel. We must tread the awful and shadowy line between censorship and freedom; between authority and democracy; between the police state and anarchy.'

The picture dimmed to be replaced by another. This was a grim-faced younger man, perhaps in his fifties. He did not look well. Dark circles were inscribed beneath his eyes and his skin lacked colour. If anything, it was the hue of nicotine-tinged fingers.

'My name is Alfonso Hunt. The year is 2142. I'm afraid that Mister Dunnett's idea of recording at regular intervals has lapsed badly. For that I apologise. I make this recording without the knowledge of my colleagues. I do so for one reason. I am dying and I wish to go on record for my own reasons.

As we approach the middle of the century, our city is not prospering as our founding fathers would have wished. There seems to have been a desire by former presidents and some consuls, including the present administration, to allow far too much freedom of the individual within this city. We still have no means of cultivating the wasteland; we still have no knowledge of cities beyond our own border and we still have a population problem. I go on the record as saying that I have been firmly opposed to the relaxing of laws that allow what I see as outrageous freedom when it comes to individual rights, whether this is in relation to religious congregation or family size. Those opposed to me will call me authoritarian but we cannot, repeat cannot allow the individual freedoms currently condoned. Some people are flaunting the law and having as many as six or seven children, without censure. Religious cults are forming and some have adopted ridiculous philosophical positions, some even suggesting that the Earth was formed as recently as the twenty first century, in spite of copious evidence to the contrary. Furthermore, other splinter and lobby groups have formed. The judicial system, which had gained respect under former administrations, has faltered now under the scepticism of the young, infected as they are by the beliefs of their foolish parents. We need a stronger police presence to quell the masses. People should have rights, but their rights should end where other people's rights begin.'

This vision too died to black. A third face appeared upon the screen. Here was a Slavic face - strong and uncompromising. She was in her sixties. Her eyes were blue and bright and she smiled through the camera towards some certain truth.

'The year is 2177. My name is President Sorensen. It has taken nearly one hundred years for this city to see the folly of its ways. We must break the bonds of human stupidity and grow our population as God wills it. Man has no right to interfere with the will of God. We must grow our population in accordance with natural laws. If we grow too many, many will die. This is God's will. All the suffering we do, we do for him, our saviour.'

This face was supplanted by a last. Here was a small, dark-haired man with a crooked nose and a strangled voice.

'The year is 2180. As you can see after listening to the last speaker, we're in a mess. The population's hittin' the half million mark and we can't feed 'em. We haven't had a scientist worth a damn since Dunnett and those we have had haven't been elected to office due to back-room deals and political manoeuvring. In fact the original idea of each member of the triumvirate coming from various levels of society has been railroaded by those who have acquired money during the course of the last century. We still can't grow food in the wasteland and we have absolutely no idea if there are any other cities in the world. So, please, if you're listening, you're a consul and you can help - for God's sake read the information you're given and bring back some sanity to this city.'

The lights sprang back to life and each of the consuls was presented with a hardcover book.

'Good luck,' said the general. And he was gone.

Elizabeth took her book, stood and left without a word.

Leslie watched her go in somewhat of a haze.

Nicholas moved close to Leslie's ear. He nodded towards Elizabeth's departing back and whispered, 'Never mix business with pleasure, my old man used to say. Especially with one of the Dawson line.'

Leslie didn't reply.

# Chapter 2

When Leslie got home, he made straight for the heater. It was only June and already his fingers were numb. As he fired up the small gas fire he looked out over Hyde Park. He was on the second floor and just beneath his window he could hear the mini prophets on their soap boxes preaching to the passers-by.

He opened the door to his postage-stamp-sized balcony and closed it behind him. He looked down. In spite of the winter chill the street was full of brown clad, shuffling humanity. Men, women and children foraged for scraps, accompanied by the orchestra of babbling voices preaching their truths, like bent messiahs, to anyone who would listen. And many were. Whole families clustered around speakers upon old milk crates, listening and nodding to recounts of the horror of their lives and of how it could all be fixed if only . . .

If only, Leslie thought: if only the original ideals of the new world had been adopted. Why weren't most people taught to read? There were books. They were limited, but there were books. He had read them. His father used to borrow them from the library and read them to him when he was just a small boy. But what good are books when people can't read? He would look into that as soon as possible. He knew that the founding fathers had intended education to be universal.

He knew about Jeremiah and Colin Dunnett and had heard of the tales of the evil Ferret. Though how much of that was urban legend remained to be seen. The only thing that he had learned from the projected presentation was that good intentions are not enough. Good government was what was needed. He sympathised with the desire for religious autonomy and he respected the right of all minority groups to be heard, but this, above all, was a time for pragmatism. Only action and sensible legislation could liberate his population. Just look at the city streets. The last consul on that video presentation had it right – things were in a mess. The city needed good schools, good hospitals and good sanitation. And he had been invested with an opportunity to help. He, Leslie Woodford, a humble second storey scientist descended directly from the Intelligentsia of the old world had risen to consul in the new one. What an honour. He would help to make the city a better place. He had always had a million ideas and only needed a forum to vent them. Now he had one. He had been voted democratically into office by the exertion of his own will. He had campaigned alone. He, alone, had made it happen. Now he was at the apex of the political process in Corporate City. It was exciting. If only his father could see him now.

As he stood, lost in thought upon his balcony, beneath him a scuffle broke out. This developed into a nasty altercation and eventually the military police were called. In a rather heavy-handed manner they dispersed the crowd and carted away the protagonists. Screams and wails of indignation went up.

He returned to the comfort of his sparse apartment. The current state of affairs would not do, he was thinking. He must be proactive. He threw himself with a bounce upon his bed and there, took up the pages of the green book he had been given. It was quite thick for a brief, he thought to himself, as he opened the well-thumbed pages.

Greetings, consul, it read – A general introduction by Sir Colin Dunnett . . .

As the twenty-first century draws to a close, we find ourselves in another Dark Age. After the bombs of 2059, a great deal of knowledge passed from human history. Alas, this loss was compounded further by the years immediately after the bombs and in particular in the days just prior to the First Triumvirate. Many of the books that had survived the war were burned and lost at that time. Those that perpetrated this, like all individuals and organisations driven by greed, ignorance and malice, belong only in the great dustbin of history. They shall not be dwelt upon here.

The post war years, under the First Triumvirate, were characterised by a great gathering and collation of that which we *did* know. The latter years of this century have seen teams of scientists and inventors probing the secrets of the technical objects that have been left to us. They have drawn schematics of everything from home computers to magnetic resonance machines; from the internal combustion engine to the turbine driven jet engine. Unfortunately, though we could, theoretically, make these many and varied objects, we do not have the raw materials to make any of them en masse. Neither do we have the ability to manufacture the various metals and plastics needed for their widespread usage.

So, Consul, we find ourselves in somewhat of a bind. We know how to make a car but we cannot make any more of them than already exist. By the time you read this preamble, hopefully this will have been remedied.

Leslie stopped reading for a moment. No, that hadn't been remedied. In fact there were no cars at all now, except in the museum. There were no planes either. There was enough oil and petrol manufactured by the city's refinery to allow production by a handful of factories, but that was all.

The arc of arable land we inhabit is still the only city of which we know, though it seems certain that if *we* have survived the bombs, then other cities must have too. However, no contact has yet been made. Radio contact has been attempted but without success, and several intrepid souls have left our shores in makeshift sailing ships, but if they have discovered other life in other lands, they have not, as yet, returned to tell their tales.

I must add that there have been some attempts to leave the city and to set up camps in the mountains, but the hardships of this are profound, given the lack of fuel and physical commodities. Most have returned after a time. Although others will no doubt try, it must be said that the present government is actively discouraging this practice. We must work together. This fracturing of the population into mountain villages plays too easily into the hands of dissidents and revolutionaries. At this early stage in the city's development the growth of such disassociated groups might prove disastrous.

Back in the city, we have uncovered, in the liberated Ground Dwellers, a great wealth of skills and we have managed quite well. We have restored limited electrical supply to the city and though we do not have the means to drill and refine fossil fuels, we are utilising the stores we already have and already some factory operations are beginning. At this stage these are principally concerned with packaging foodstuffs and in the manufacture of basic drugs.

To the west our city limits now extend to just beyond Parramatta, where many older structures from the century before last were found unscathed. Mercifully, the old Westmead Hospital has somehow survived to help supplement the already overcrowded St Vincent's, Royal North Shore and Royal Prince Alfred hospitals that service the inner city. There are many growing communities springing up on the northern beaches and to the south the wasteland begins beyond the old refinery at Kernel. Beyond these reaches our scientists have been unable, as yet, to cultivate one blade of living grass in its devastated soil. Hopefully, this too will soon be redressed.

The last twenty years or so have been fraught with problems - some of them expected: some not. Feeding and housing our population has been a burden; keeping sufficient infrastructure and gainful employment, another. The triumvirate keeps its control through the loyalty of the military and so far, this has been consistent. A rudimentary economy, partly based on barter, has arisen. This has unfortunately been usurped by some for their own gain. Some citizens, it seems, availed themselves of wealth after the fall of Jeremiah's initial government and sought to use this to curry favour in the new order. Though we try to stamp it out, bribery and corruption are still a part of everyday dealings. Perpetrators are punished, but there is more below the surface than above the water line.

Our administration has been taken by surprise, however, by the speed with which splinter groups, both political and social, have sprung up in the last two decades. At this time there are already a dozen church groups vying for the hearts and souls of our citizens. Other lobby groups have also quickly evolved and everyone, it seems, sees their own self-interest as paramount - even if this threatens the stability of the whole structure. Many of our citizens seem to feel that individual rights outweigh the good of the whole, so much so that the military has been used to crush several riots in the city over recent years. The challenge of our government is to balance the rights of each of these groups whilst maintaining a unified whole. Our objective has been to allow individual freedom, where possible - but too often individuals have taken generosity for weakness. Recently, a cult of men and women was put on trial and executed for crimes perpetrated upon another cult. The decision to execute, though regrettable, is one of the many harsh realities with which any government in the coming years will face.

Whatever the case, in whatever kind of world this message finds you, the information in it should be of some assistance. As a consul from the ranks of the Intelligentsia you have been given more information than the other consul. These are drawings, charts and schematics that might help you in your quest for technological advancement. If it is within your power to use this information for the good of the city, do so. But beware of those who would use this information to further self-interest at the expense of others.

As one of the two consuls, you will be asked to give advice to the president and to make important and sometimes highly difficult decisions. At times, the president and your fellow consul will not agree with you and your fervent wishes may be overturned. There is no cabinet or committee to fall back upon. Remember, the president has the final right of pass or veto. Such is the nature of this centralised democracy. But you must respect the process, whether or not any one particular argument you have made has won the day.

Good fortune, consul.

C.D.

Leslie ran his tongue over his lips in anticipation. He turned over the page and to his delight there were notes and snippets from past thinkers and from Dunnett himself on the general precepts of good government and on the legislative apparatus that his triumvirate had set up and put in place a century ago. He had thoughtfully compiled whatever information he had at his disposal in this booklet. Snatches from the Communist Manifesto by Marx (approach with caution); notes on the free market economy (approach with equal caution); some passages from Mein Kampf (disregard completely) and a plethora of chapters from philosophical and political writings from Plato to Aristotle; from Descartes to Russell; from Machiavelli to Onslow and from Churchill to Gandhi. Anything, it seemed that Dunnett could get his hands on that seemed worthy of note for a would-be governor.

But it was with tremulous fingers that he turned to the back part of the book which had the scientific and technical information which he so craved. He turned expectantly to the last part of the book and found . . .

Nothing.

The outside margins were intact but someone had taken to the pages with a knife and meticulously cut out the entire contents. What remained was an ignorant hole mocked by equally ignorant borders. A neatly cut out square chasm revealed the inside of the back hardcover of the book an inch or so below. Glued onto that surface was a printed note saying: 'The offending material has been removed.'

Leslie rose all in one movement from the bed. He found himself standing beside it as if awakening from a bad dream. His breath was short and his eyes wide. What did this mean? What had become of Dunnett's notes? Who was responsible for this ghastly act? He must find out. It could not wait until tomorrow. He must find out – now.

*

Fifteen minutes later, it was a rather wet Leslie who entered the foyer of the AWA building in York Street. He buzzed on the intercom, carefully watched by two burly security guards, and was soon a dozen floors up, walking into Nicholas Brand's apartment, apologising for the water he was recklessly depositing out of his raincoat and onto Brand's carpet.

'Why didn't you bring an umbrella?' asked Nicholas.

'I did,' Leslie replied, reaching behind him and holding up the brolly he had rested in the corridor before entering. 'It's raining cats and dogs out there.'

'Come in,' said Nicholas with a grin. 'Leave your coat on the stand.'

A young man, in his late teens, popped his head around the corner. 'You alright, Dad?' he asked.

'I'm fine, son. Come and meet my fellow consul,' Nicholas replied. 'Leslie, this is Edgar.'

'Hi.' Edgar greeted him politely with a handshake. He was thinner than his father and taller. He had brown hair and dark eyes like his Dad, but he appeared to be more the strong, athletic type.

'I know what you're thinking,' said Nicholas with a laugh. 'He does take more after his mother. Please, sit down.'

Soon all the pleasantries were done, Edgar had returned to his room and Leslie was sipping thoughtfully on a cup of tea.

'So?' asked Nicholas.

In response, Leslie abandoned his tea and foraged under his thick woollen jumper. He produced the book and placed it on the table. It was unscathed and dry.

'Do you think it's such a good idea to carry state secrets around with you?' Nicholas asked. 'Especially in this weather?'

'Take a look at the book,' said Leslie. 'Do you notice anything about it?'

Nicholas picked it up. 'It's thicker than the one I got,' he noted as he weighed it in his hand.

'Take a look inside,' said Leslie with a nod.

'But it would be, wouldn't it?' Nicholas mused, 'You have all that other scientific stuff to deal with as well.' As he spoke, he thumbed through the pages. He soon discovered the loss.

He screwed up his face into a small ball of disdain, as if he had just eaten a bad oyster. 'What in blazes?'

'What do you make of it?' asked Leslie with a quick, nervous sip of his tea. He looked carefully for Nicholas' response.

Nicholas' eyes widened. 'My father warned me about this sort of thing. He used to say that censorship was the death of the human spirit.' He looked again at the note: 'Offending material,' he muttered.

'What do you suggest we do?' asked Leslie, at least convinced for the moment that Nicholas was as surprised as he was at the vandalism.

'I say we meet with President Dawson first thing tomorrow,' he replied.

'Surely this could only have been done by a former office holder?' suggested Leslie. 'Who else could gain access?'

'That's what we need to find out,' replied Nicholas.

'My money's on the last woman we saw in the presentation. She sounded like a likely candidate.'

'Hold your horses there, Les,' Nicholas replied, jarring Leslie with the liberty of this familiarity, 'we don't know anything yet.'

'We simply must find those papers,' said Leslie, dejectedly.

'Don't worry, we'll find them,' Nicholas reassured him with a quick pat on the back.

But Leslie wasn't so sure.

*

As he entered his apartment in the World Square skyscraper in George Street, Damien was in a foul temper. He wasn't sure why; he was just in a bad mood.

He noticed that he often was when the moon was full. In fact, he wasn't even sure that the moon was full. He hadn't seen it for a month, courtesy of this ridiculous weather. But he felt that it must be full because when it was, he always felt like he had an itchiness inside him that he couldn't scratch. Violently, he shook out his raincoat in the hall.

He shooed a cat out of the way as he entered his penthouse. How the hell any cats had survived the days after the bombs, God only knew. But somehow, they had. Some rich people had obviously bred cats in their scraper apartments after the war and managed to hide them from the post-war city long enough for them not to get eaten. Probably lots of people had, because now, somehow, there were thousands of the feline menaces creeping through the scrapers. You never saw any in the streets though, he mused. They were obviously pretty good eating.

He shut the door to his apartment, threw his raincoat recklessly towards a coat stand, knocking it over, and made his way towards the drinks cabinet. He downed a quick beer and opened another before he settled down enough to look around his room.

Languidly he made his way towards the window. He looked out towards the west, but the night was glum and the view unrewarding. He kicked a coffee table without vigour and sat at his desk. He flicked, without purpose, through a cheap street-produced porn magazine and then stared out of the window for a while. He felt bored and he felt lonely.

He pulled out Elizabeth Dawson's card from his pocket and looked at it. He thought about her pretty face and a faraway look washed across his face. He had met her once when he was a little boy. He remembered her apartment. It was a rich person's apartment – high up in the clouds. Her father was a very important man. He was the president at the time. She was very rich and she was very pretty in a bright blue frock and matching ribbons. He had a few memories of that day. They all revolved around Elizabeth. He remembered that she teased him about having sandy coloured hair and being too skinny. The usual kids' stuff. But there was something else; something else on the edge of his memory he couldn't quite excavate. His father was there on some kind of business, he remembered. But it was something to do with Elizabeth. No. It wouldn't come. The memory would not dislodge.

He looked back at her card and idly turned it over so that its back was exposed. There was a message on it: Meet me at my office - tomorrow midday.

# Chapter 3

Nicholas and Leslie entered the same room in which Robert had first met Jeremiah over a century before. The room was redecorated in pastels and the walls adorned with paintings. The décor was chunkier in the late twenty second century style but it was the same room – worktable to the left, lounge and coffee table to the right; a spectacular view of the city scrapers all around.

Elizabeth rose to meet them. The three shook hands and together they sat on, almost in, the soft leather couch.

'So we're straight to work, I see?' She smiled, but that smile begged a question. Why are you here at this hour - nine am on our first Monday in office?

'Sorry to turn up so suddenly,' Nicholas apologised, 'but Leslie's discovered a problem with his notes.'

'A problem?'

'Yes,' Nicholas qualified. 'He hasn't got any.'

'Leslie?' she questioned.

'Yes,' he stammered, once again struck by Elizabeth's beauty. 'I'm very worried.'

He handed her the book and soon the quizzical expression that had spread across Nicholas' face the night before, washed across hers.

'This can't be right,' she mumbled. She reached for the phone. 'Get Stefan,' she ordered.

In the several minutes between command and compliance Nicholas and Elizabeth chatted. They apparently had known one another for some time. From their conversation Leslie learned that Elizabeth had been educated in Scraper 8 at a time when Nicholas had been teaching there. He also heard how Elizabeth's family was very wealthy and that her family had already produced several consuls and one president over the last century.

Elizabeth had an impeccable pedigree. Leslie was thinking about how lovely her voice was, when, unexpectedly, she asked him, 'So, Consul Woodford, what do you make out of all of this?'

He wasn't sure what to make of it, but he was very disturbed by it, as he told her. Both Nicholas and Elizabeth nodded grave agreement. This was unprecedented, she told him, but she felt quite sure that everything would be sorted out.

Before long, a young man with thinning, but long sandy-blond hair, fine chiselled bird-like features, a small craggy nose and close-set eyes, entered carrying a suitcase. He wore a beautifully cut, beige suit and was efficiently effeminate in his movements.

'This is Stefan,' Elizabeth explained. 'He is my personal secretary and our accounts man. He accounts for everything from how much money we have in our coffers, to matters of missing laundry.'

Elizabeth patted Stefan's hand. The two shared an esoteric laugh and let the mystery lie there.

Leslie noted the familiarity and was jealous, without reason.

Stefan looked at the book and his expression showed great surprise. 'I'll have the police look into how this happened,' he said with concern. 'I apologise, Consul Woodford, for the great inconvenience. Fortunately, the original document is housed in the great vault in Macquarie Street. I'll have it copied and sent to you later today.'

Leslie was greatly relieved and pleased. He told the young man so. Soon the efficient, sandy-haired young man was on his way.

'I'm busy today, consuls,' said Elizabeth, as they parted. 'I'm sure that you have offices to set up and staff to meet? I remember what my first weeks in office were like. We're scheduled to meet for our first policy meeting tomorrow in the government buildings. So I'll see you both then.' She turned to Leslie, 'Once you've had a chance to read your manuscript.'

She smiled and with a handshake and a closing door, she was gone.

'You should make it a little more obvious next time,' said Nicholas as they descended in the elevator.

Leslie did a slight double take but he did not remonstrate. He realised that his affection for Elizabeth was transparent. He had always been a terrible dissembler and a worse liar. He simply accepted the gentle rebuke as it was intended – a friendly barb. But he was also aware that Nicholas was making an important point in a friendly manner: his connection with both Nicholas and Elizabeth was a work arrangement and an important one at that. He must control his feelings.

The two parted and made their separate ways to their offices above Macquarie Street. Leslie was ill at ease on two counts. One, he couldn't imagine how he was going to spend six years in the company of Elizabeth Dawson without, at some stage, expressing his devotion to her and probably making a fool of himself in the process and two, he was very worried about who had cut the heart out of such an important document as the green book and how on Earth they were able to do so without some complicity with others. If there was a conspiracy then . . . but no, he didn't believe in conspiracy theories. 99.9% of the time they were populist nonsense and the other 0.1% they were simply nonsense. Everything would be alright. The police would catch the fanatic who had ripped the pages out of his book and they would be brought to justice. They would be punished.

That was how the world worked.

*

Damien was in a much better frame of mind, than he had been the night before, when he walked into Elizabeth Dawson's office. He was let in before she arrived and sauntered around the room looking into boxes of photographs and memorabilia that were soon to adorn the walls. He moved with the simple grace of a country boy, which must have come from some genetic throwback because there hadn't been such a species for a long, long while. He was peering inquisitively at a pile of books on the consul's desk when a voice came from behind him.

'I shouldn't worry,' she said from the door, 'there are no microphones in here.'

He turned guiltily and released the small pile of papers in his hand. 'I didn't . . .' he began.

She lounged against the doorway with her dark hair cascading like a frozen waterfall about her smiling face. The crystal pools of her eyes shone brightly. 'Don't worry. You won't uncover any state secrets.' She sashayed lightly into the room. 'Take a seat, Damien.'

He complied and she sat opposite him. His body language was tense. He was uncertain of her; wary and guarded.

'I see you received my message?'

He nodded. 'Yeah. How can I help you?'

'I believe that your father knew mine, back in the seventies. It seems that Damien Enterprises and government officials have been consorting, at least covertly, for some time.'

'I remember your apartment.'

'Do you?'

'Yeah.'

'Do you remember me?' She opened her eyes flirtatiously.

'I remember you when you were very little.'

'Do you now? And what was your impression?'

Damien knew how to handle women. He knew that he must not only be polite at this point but also intentionally flattering. 'You were as beautiful then as you are now,' he replied.

Elizabeth laughed, 'Well said,' she said and her eyes were bright with mischief. 'We must talk further of it - some time.'

But that 'some time' was not now. This was the scripted end of the small talk. They both knew it. Damien was waiting for a question. He had no idea why she had invited him, possibly as her first official duty of this administration, to discuss . . . what?

'I know, off the record, that you and your family have a great deal of power in this town and that you can get things done with a minimum of fuss,' Elizabeth began. 'The several factories you operate provide this city with a good deal of its creature comforts.'

He sat quietly back into his chair. There was still no question. He listened with interest.

In a subconscious move to counter his motion back into his chair, Elizabeth leaned forward across her brightly polished, wooden desk and said quietly, 'Apart from my assigned staff, I can, in my second term, choose an adviser at my discretion. You come highly recommended, Damien. My father watched you grow. If he were alive today, I know that he would approve of you as my choice as chief adviser. What do you say?'

Finally - a question. Damien looked at her intensely for a moment or two, raised his head and stared beyond her charismatic beauty and out through the window.

She sat back into her chair, allowing him his space.

'Look, thanks anyway, Miss Dawson,' he eventually replied, 'but I'm not your man. I was never a team player and the thought of working with your consuls doesn't interest me in the least. Thanks for your interest though.'

He rose to leave. She responded by stopping him

with her voice. 'I'll make it worth your while.'

He stared at her across the desk and saw her framed like an angel by the backlight of the window. He almost laughed at his negativity, but he stayed firm.

'No, I'm sorry,' he answered. He moved back towards her desk and he took her hand in his. 'It's nothing personal, Miss Dawson. But one way to 'get things done, as you put it, is in anonymity and what you're asking will compromise that. Government officials need transparency. I'm a businessman, not a politician.'

'That's why I ask for your help. Will you at least consider it?'

'I'll think about it,' he replied. He kissed her hand lightly and with great chivalry. Then he turned and left her with a smile.

She lingered above her desk and watched him leave. Then she sat and tapped her fingers upon that desk in silent thought.

Elizabeth was a young woman used to getting her own way. She must rethink her approach.

*

Leslie was introduced to his secretary. He was a little, balding man with thick glasses, attached to super-sized ears that projected mercilessly towards opposing walls. His face was rounded like an apologetic full moon. What little side hair he possessed had been combed over the top of his head in a forlorn and misguided attempt to disguise his follicle deficiency. He wore a white shirt and black tie, both of which were tucked into a pair of tailored, khaki shorts, held up by black braces that drew broad, parallel lines from tummy to shoulders. These drew his shorts up higher than they needed to be, giving him a comical appearance. Below this striking ensemble he sported long white socks and finally, sandals. His body language conveyed immense timidity. He offered a weak handshake and averted his eyes to the floor.

'Nice to meet you, Mark,' said Leslie as they met.

Mark merely nodded with his eyes still fixed downward.

Leslie tried again. 'I look forward to getting to know you over the next few years.'

But again Mark only nodded and shuffled.

It seemed to Leslie that it might be a long few years if the present conversation was anything to go by. But then the phone rang.

Like a man possessed, Mark sprang into action. He grabbed the phone, started a small tape machine connected to it and, with newfound authority, answered.

'Consul Woodford's office. Who may I ask is calling? (Pause) No, I'm sorry, sir, but the consul is not available for interviews at this time. (Pause) Yes, sir, I'll let you know. Good day.'

He sat immediately at his desk and typed something at hyper-speed into his computer. He explained as he typed.

'I take down the details of every caller, sir,' he explained to his new boss, 'including an exact typed transcript of the conversation, which I also audio tape for later verification. I date and file every tape individually.' He nodded his head towards a distant room within which Leslie could just make out rows of Dictaphone tapes flourishing upon the walls. 'At times I may take the liberty of not bothering you with calls that will, in all probability, waste your time. I've not missed a day's work in twelve years. In that time I have served Consuls Collette and Dawson. They found me to be satisfactory, sir, and I hope that you will also.'

Leslie laughed with delight and was so impressed that he stopped Mark's typing to shake his hand a second time. 'It doesn't matter how good the boss is, Mark. Without a good secretary, he's nothing.'

Mark, who had once again shrivelled into his former timidity, nodded silent agreement and twitched a smile of pleasure at the compliment.

The phone rang again, and again Mark powered into action. But this time he listened. This time the call was of a different nature. Mark was not so dismissive.

'He'll be there immediately,' was all he said.

A few minutes later, Leslie was entering the government building across the road from his office. He was followed by Mark, who held a clipboard in one hand and a pen in the other. Protruding from his top pocket was an active Dictaphone.

Leslie swept back his hair, wet from the rain. With one deft sweep, Mark removed the water from the minimal strands of hair residing upon his cranium. Leslie noted this and thought it to be the one advantage of baldness.

'My apologies, consul,' said Stefan, advancing on them with two hulking guards behind. He appeared flustered. 'Please step this way.'

Stefan closed the door on the guards and approached Leslie and his secretary. Mark had his pen poised.

'I don't know where to begin,' said Stefan. He was obviously flustered and far less controlled than he had been in Elizabeth's office not long before. His thin hair was fractionally askew and his beige suit not quite so impeccably creaseless. 'Something outside of the ordinary has occurred.'

Leslie looked towards Mark, who was much more used to such affairs. Mark, back in confident mode, finished scribbling onto his notepad and looked back towards Stefan for further information.

'You see,' Stefan continued, brushing back his

falling fringe and looking nowhere in particular, 'the second . . . the original manuscript . . . it seems, has also been misplaced.'

These last words he shunted out in a rush, so as to minimise the negative impact.

It didn't work.

'What!' Leslie exclaimed.

'Now, now, calm down,' assuaged Stefan. 'I'm sure there will be some logical explanation.'

'I'm sure there will be,' Leslie responded, 'or plenty of people are going to lose their jobs.'

This struck a deep note in Stefan, 'No. No, consul, we will sort this out. I promise you.'

'Who the hell is in charge of this ship?' asked Leslie, outraged beyond the fringes of his usual self.

'I assure you, consul that . . .'

Fortunately for Stefan the cavalry arrived just in time - in the form of Elizabeth Dawson.

'I've just heard,' she said, leaving behind her one very solid man, apparently her minder. He was soaked but efficiently shook out the umbrella that had protected his boss. She shut him out with the clang of the door. 'What do you know, Stefan?'

All eyes were upon the young man.

He took in a deep breath, 'It seems that somehow the . . .' he gulped, 'the original manuscript, containing the blueprints for the Sciences, has been misplaced.'

'Misplaced?' echoed Leslie, in disbelief.

'We will find them, I assure you,' replied Stefan, with closed eyes and a movement of his hand that suggested an imaginary patting down of invisible matter encroaching about his mid-riff.

'What do you know?' asked Elizabeth, in an emphatic but constrained tone.

He responded with an uneven hoarseness in his voice, 'We're currently reviewing everyone who's had any access to the book.'

'You must be joking?' replied Leslie, his dark eyes incredulous and searching. 'How can something like this happen? There must be copies of such vital information elsewhere?'

'It's not as simple as that,' Stefan replied. 'It was expressly stated by our founding fathers that the confidentiality of these documents be kept from those who might seek to use the information they contain for their own ends.'

'That's all very well,' Leslie countered, 'but there must be other copies of such invaluable documents?'

'I know how it seems to you, sir,' said Stefan, 'but I am the chief overseer of all information held by the state and I'm telling you, these documents were copied only once for consuls and the originals kept here, under strict guard.'

'Strict guard,' grunted Leslie.

'When were they last copied, before the copy was given to Consul Woodford?' asked Elizabeth.

'Not for nearly thirty years,' Stefan replied, miserably. 'That was the last time a consul was of scientific expertise. No other consul has needed them.'

Leslie was growing angry. 'Are you telling me that the most significant papers of the century have been 'misplaced, and that they haven't been considered by government for nearly thirty years?'

'Please don't shoot the messenger, sir,' replied Stefan with his head bowed and his hands raised. 'In my lifetime there has never been a consul well versed in the Sciences. I don't run things. I simply account for them.'

Leslie saw the sense in this. The young man wasn't responsible but he had to take his indignation out on someone. The whole thing was preposterous.

'My family has been in politics for a long time, Consul Woodford,' said Elizabeth in Stefan's defence.

'What Stefan says is true. The art of Science, if that is the correct way of putting it, has been lost over the last century. Our education system is in dire need of repair as I'm sure you'll agree?'

Leslie was getting agitated. 'Of course I agree, but that's hardly the point.'

'Calm down, Consul,' Elizabeth rebuked him quietly.

He lowered his voice, but did not diminish his passion, 'What are we going to do? We must find at least one of the manuscripts.'

'It's unlikely that whoever has them will be able to use them effectively because no one . . .' Stefan began.

'Is taught Science anymore,' Leslie completed the sentence for him. 'Yes. I know. You've already said that, Stefan. But I haven't spent my whole life reading whatever I could get my hands on to be denied the major prize. I can use those documents. I know I'll be able to help Corporate City if I can just get my hands on the damn things. This is so frustrating and infuriating!' Leslie had heaped up his speech into an impressive crescendo. He quieted his voice to complete the effect. 'So Stefan, President Dawson has already assured us that you are the fix-it man. I suggest that you go and fix it.'

There was silence for a moment then Stefan replied, 'I'll call the police.' And he made for the door.

'That would be a good start,' Leslie muttered as the beige but dishevelled vision of Stefan made its hasty exit.

Leslie became aware that his cheeks were puffed and hot and that his adrenaline was a river of fire rushing through him. He suddenly felt ashamed.

'I'm sorry I lost my temper,' he apologised. 'But you must agree that this is ridiculous?'

'There's no need to apologise, Consul Woodford,' she replied with surprise in her voice. 'It's wonderful to be working with such a passionate man. I had no idea.'

Leslie looked up at her to see if she was mocking him. She didn't seem to be. She appeared to be completely sincere and genuinely impressed. Her dark hair and sparkling blue-green eyes drank him in, and, for a brief moment, he enjoyed rapture. He had made a good impression on Elizabeth Dawson. Well and good. But for the moment that was a secondary concern. 'We must find at least one copy of that book,' he stated, as if saying this would somehow make it a certainty.

'We have rudimentary surveillance,' she replied. 'And Stefan is a very competent civil servant, in spite of what you might think. Don't worry, consul, we'll get them back. It seems that there's finally someone in this city competent enough to make use of them.' She took his arm and secretly, he shuddered inside. 'Come join me under an umbrella?'

The two walked through the door and into the foyer where Elizabeth's large minder stood ready with an unfurled umbrella. Now he had to escort both of them. They only had to go just across the street but it was raining in torrents and he had just dried himself off.

Mark turned off his Dictaphone and placed it into the pocket of his shorts to protect it from the rain. He made a quick dash back across Macquarie Street but misjudged the gutter and ended up with a soggy white sock in a drowned sandal. He would have cursed, but Mark didn't curse.

*

Late that evening Elizabeth sat behind her desk, speaking into a recording device: 'We must maintain control at a government level,' she said. 'Lobby groups must be curtailed where they threaten the good of the city.'

She stopped the recording device and stared out at the rain.

# Chapter 4

Damien woke up with a pretty, young woman asleep on his chest but with Elizabeth Dawson on his mind. He listened to the quiet rhythm of the girl's breathing. He felt it soft upon his breast. He stared up at the ceiling and he thought.

What was it about Elizabeth that intrigued him so? Obviously, she was beautiful. But there was something else. Some hidden presence was there. Some dark and secret thing lurked inside of her and he wanted to prize it out like a pearl from its shell. He was mad at himself. She had offered him the means to get close to her but he had refused. Was it too late? Probably not . . . but what was he thinking? He must resist. He knew that. Sure, he was a businessman in a world that only had rudimentary business but, even so, he couldn't be involved with the Dawson family. They were well known for their political connections and he didn't want to align with any particular political group. All he wanted to do was increase his earnings by increasing the number of citizens with the means to buy. He needed consumers. He needed people with money or the equivalent. He checked himself. He was putting the horse before the cart. Even if all of the citizens of Corporate City had the means to buy endless products, what would they buy? He needed product first. And for this he needed raw material and many more factories and distribution centres; all of these things he must have before a consumer even entered the market. It was all so far away. Just a dream. Unless . . .

That Woodford guy. He had heard that he was a smart one. He had purportedly fashioned a rudimentary telescope from smelted recycled glass. He had heard that he had made a short-range walkie-talkie when he was only in his teens and that, not long after, he had been invited to the local museum, where he had turned a pile of bones, hitherto stored in a box in the dim recesses of the building, that the superintendent of the place had suspected might be important, into a full skeleton of a Tyrannosaur. This specimen was incredible as the only one of its kind known in existence after the lootings and destruction after the bombs of a hundred years ago. It was a physical challenge to the growing theory, espoused just over a decade ago, that the Earth had only come into existence in the last two hundred years.

He should have spoken with Woodford. He realised that now. He should have spoken with Woodford at the party but, as usual, his natural distaste for competition had stopped him.

The same thoughts dogged him later that morning as he entered the business section of his skyscraper apartment and looked at the map of an imaginary future Corporate City plastered across the wall. He had had an artist draw it there and it had been well drawn. He called it his 'wish map'. It showed the city centre and its surrounds as Damien would like it to be. Stretching out towards what he had dubbed the Parramatta Line, a series of factories was drawn, just on the edge of the wasteland. It showed the city centre and then, fanning out away from it was the arable land before the radiation affected wasteland. From Palm Beach in the north to Parramatta in the west to Kernel in the south, all dotted with factories that he imagined producing everything from motor cars to canned goods. He envisioned a city population catching some form of public transport to work in these factories. He imagined them earning enough money to buy the goods produced. He imagined a basic economy. Not this two-status, hotchpotch that existed now. And in his wildest imaginings, he dreamed of international trade; of imports and exports: of real 'big business'.

The more he thought, the more he realised. He didn't need Elizabeth Dawson; he didn't need political affiliation. He had been right to resist her charms. He needed scientific know-how. The business world, the *whole* world, he suddenly saw, was limited without the scientist, the inventor. They conceived of the world and then the engineers constructed it. The businessman and the consumer, the end user, only lubricated its wheels. Businessmen had nothing to sell and people had nowhere to work without the thinkers and their input. It became clear to him – he must speak with Woodford.

However, it was not Woodford, but Dawson, who chose that moment to enter his apartment.

'Sorry to interrupt,' said Elizabeth, hanging elegantly by the door. 'May I come in?'

The answer was obvious and soon the two found themselves admiring the imaginary city on Damien's wall.

'I see the existing factories here,' she pointed to the map at the outskirts of the central city, 'but what are these ones in a ring further out towards the wasteland?'

'They're the factories I intend to build one day. They'll eventually supplant the ones in existence now,' he replied, looking at the map but noticing, more than anything, the delightful aroma of Elizabeth's hair. 'We'll need to transport the workers out there of course, but if we can manage it, we can provide useful work for most of the street dwellers.'

'You're a visionary,' she muttered to herself, but loudly enough so that Damien could hear.

At that moment he so much wanted to be a visionary, just so that he could fit the picture of him she appeared to be forming in her head, but he had to be honest.

'No,' he admitted, 'this is my father's idea. I just had an artist paint it upon my wall so I never forget it.'

'That shows vision,' replied Elizabeth, turning the beacon of her bright eyes upon him.

'Perhaps,' he returned, though a little unsteadily, smote by the rigour of her eyes. He looked back to the wall and added, 'If we had the means we might even be able to make use of the mountains.'

'It's illegal to live in the mountains, young man. You know that,' Elizabeth replied, playfully.

'I meant in the future,' replied Damien.

'I know you said that you can't work for me,' she said, 'and I accept that, but I wonder if, perhaps, you might consider working with Leslie Woodford?'

Damien was aghast. All of the thoughts he had entertained over the past few hours had suddenly borne fruition, as if the gods had been listening in and rewarded his desire.

'I'd like to meet him,' he replied.

Elizabeth looked at his delicious, slender body that even a rustic baggy shirt couldn't completely disguise. She took quick inventory of his fine but strong features and she sighed.

'I'll arrange it,' she said.

And she was gone in a dark swirling mass of unbridled hair and feline, tight-bodied elegance.

Damien sighed. He sensed the double-edged sword of opportunity and danger lurking in every stride of that young woman.

And he heard the sirens calling.

*

Leslie had spent a sleepless night. Unlike Damien, he didn't have a young woman to pass the time, or an orgasm to act as a sedative. He had stayed wide awake for the majority of the night, enjoying only brief, broken spats of dreamtime. And what sleep he had managed was a compendium of missing manuscripts and Elizabeth Dawson's rubescent cheeks. Her dark hair ripped like a tornado through his mind and the pages of his precious manuscript were sucked up into its vortex towards the oblivion of the sky in a thousand loose-leaf pages.

He was dark-eyed and dishevelled when he found his way into a meeting with Nicholas Brand and Elizabeth Dawson the following morning.

'My God. What happened to you?' asked Nicholas as Leslie entered the meeting room.

He didn't have a chance to answer before Elizabeth arrived. She was dressed in a brown business suit and perfectly presented. She had not a hair out of place. Her makeup was subtle but charming. She was perfect in every way. If someone had designed the scene to juxtapose dishevelment and tight regimentation of appearance, he or she could not have illustrated it better than the contrast between the two.

'My God,' she started, after she sat and raised her eyes to greet the two men. 'What on Earth happened to you?'

'That's what I just asked him,' said Nicholas with a smile.

'Nothing serious,' Leslie replied. 'I just couldn't sleep thinking about those stolen manuscripts.'

'Any progress?' asked Nicholas.

Elizabeth placed her fingers on the desk. 'I have one piece of bad news, but,' she emphasised, before Leslie could enter any complaint, 'it's not the end of the world. Not yet.'

'What do you mean?' asked Leslie.

'One of the manuscripts has definitely been destroyed.'

'What?' muttered Leslie, rather pathetically. He was too tired to be angry. He had imagined the worst all night and now the worst had come. He was enervated with fatigue.

'Before you get upset, Consul Woodford, this first manuscript was the one cut from your book and it was fairly easy to trace. It was stolen by Consul Sorensen who had her own agenda, it seems. We all saw her in the video tape two nights ago. You recall, she is somewhat enamoured with the idea that God hates technology and that man is essentially bad.'

'I told you,' said Leslie to Nicholas.

Nicholas shrugged in defeat.

'She admitted as much to the police last night. Make no mistake, she and her fellow cult members will be dealt with severely. But as for the other, the original manuscript, we haven't given up hope on that yet.'

'I've been thinking about that,' said Leslie. 'Surely there was a digital copy. I can't imagine Sir Colin Dunnett leaving only two copies of such a vitally important manuscript. He must have had it on a computer somewhere?'

'Look, that may be the case,' she replied, reaching her hand across the desk and placing her hand palm-down upon his, 'but if he did, we have absolutely no record of it. As far as we know, there are only the two . . .' she checked herself, '. . . only the *one* copy in existence. But, and this is the good news, Consul Sorensen swears that neither she, nor the group that she represents know anything about the other copy.'

'How can you be so certain that they're telling the truth?' Leslie asked.

'We have our methods,' Elizabeth replied cryptically.

'When was it last sighted?' asked Nicholas.

'What do you mean?' asked Elizabeth.

'When was the original manuscript last seen?' he repeated.

Elizabeth paused for a moment. 'I don't know, exactly,' she replied, brushing her delightful fringe away from her forehead. 'But I assume that it was accounted for regularly.'

'Well, when was it last accounted for?' asked Leslie, picking up the scent.

'I see what you mean,' muttered Elizabeth thoughtfully. She picked up the phone. 'Stefan,' she began, 'find out when the original manuscript we're looking for was last sighted. (Pause) No, I mean actually seen; touched. (Pause) Very well.' She put down the phone. 'Funny,' she said with a faraway smile, 'but that hadn't even occurred to me.'

In fact, it took more than three hours for the answer to arrive and by that time Elizabeth, Nicholas and Leslie were taking lunch.

Stefan appeared in another beige suit. He looked like a messenger bearing bad news. He was hesitant to enter the room in which the trio ate and, even after he was spied at the door by Elizabeth, he tarried for a moment or two as if uncertain whether to enter, or to flee.

'Whatever is it?' Elizabeth quizzed him as he tentatively entered the lunchroom. She almost laughed at the fearful expression etched upon his face.

'Can I see you alone for a moment?' he asked Elizabeth.

'Certainly not,' she replied in a strikingly defiant tone. 'Anything you have to say to me can be said in front of my two consuls.'

Stefan fully entered the room and was laid to siege by three pairs of eyes: Elizabeth's bright and beautiful, Nicholas' dark and inquisitive and Leslie's, searching and troubled.

'I'm sorry to tell you . . .' he began.

'I don't want to hear this!' Leslie erupted. 'If you're about to tell me that the other manuscript has been burned or butchered or taken up to God or whatever, I don't want to hear it!'

This outburst made quite an impression on everyone in the room, especially Stefan, who looked towards Elizabeth as if he was choking on a bone.

'Well, Stefan?' asked Elizabeth.

'It appears,' he began in a sort of whining, sycophantic noise that seemed to emanate more through his nose than from his mouth, 'that the original manuscript has not, in fact, been actually *seen* for . . . fifty-two years.'

This news broke like the first lightning of a storm upon the unwary traveller. The trio reacted with a collective, 'What?'

Stefan gathered in his breath and continued bravely, 'It hasn't ever been needed. The last consul who was even a scientist was elected a little over thirty years ago. But, you see, the copy that he had was the same one given to Leslie, or rather *not* given to Leslie. There's been no need to even think about the original until this one went missing. It was always assumed that it was safe in the government vault.'

Stefan cringed, as if a dog about to be struck. He bundled up one eye into a crease and held his head down to one side. He was trying to shield himself from the oncoming thunder. But it did not come.

Elizabeth and Nicholas were silent and contemplative. Perhaps they were waiting for Leslie to initiate the storm, for they both looked at him.

Eventually, he spoke in a measured and controlled voice. 'Am I to understand,' he whispered, 'that the most significant document we have in our limited civilisation's possession has not only been lost, but has been considered so insignificant that it has not even been sighted for half a century?'

That seemed to sum it up pretty well, for Stefan uttered not one sound.

'Well, that is incredible.' He shook his head. 'That is absolutely gob-smacking. To think that the powers that have been in control of this city over the past half century have seen so little value in scientific progress that they have not had multiple copies of the original made during that time; to think that the various governments of Corporate City during that period have been negligent of that fundamental duty. I mean, look at the place. Ninety percent of it is a cesspool of curdled milk and the cream's making all the rules. We haven't had a scientist in office for the last three decades. And wasn't that the original idea of the triumvirate of power? Representation and progress for all?'

He waited for a response but none came. Nicholas and Elizabeth listened with interest and Stefan appeared nervous.

'Dunnett understood that the way out of the mire was through science.' He repeated it to make his point more savagely and his voice began to rise. 'Science, - the method of inquiry that never takes itself too seriously; the methodology that willingly throws any hypothesis away when a better, more useful theory presents itself; the thinking man's religion. All of this has been thrown away in less than one hundred years? I can't believe it. I can't believe that human beings could ever be so stupid!' He was getting passionate again. 'Here we are, fellow Corporate City-Siders, in one city alone in the possibility of a sea of others but, if they exist, we know nothing of them. They may be there but we can't contact them. There may be other economies but we can't trade with them. Why? Because we have allowed superstition to lead us into the safety of certainty - into the dangerous waters of certainty! Tell me this, Stefan, why do you think the Roman Empire at the time of Christ had tap water and sewage while the streets of London fifteen hundred years later had none? Why were they dumping their shit into the streets while the Ancient Romans were flushing it away?'

Stefan didn't know, or if he did, he said nothing.

'I'll tell you why, Stefan, I'll tell you *all* why. It was because the Dark Ages intervened in Europe. It was because ignorance intervened. It was because when you don't understand anything you have two choices: you can either run away scared, create a superstition, call it magic, or the will of God, or whatever you like, or you can enquire into its nature; try to understand it; reveal its secrets, bit by argumentative bit, on a road that never has the satisfaction of an end. This is the scientific method. It's a thorny and troublesome road but it's a road that leads to knowledge rather than a road which leads to self-satisfied ignorance. When humans fully embrace religious doctrine, they don't have to think because their doctrine is firm and unyielding. The religious zealot thinks the same thing at eighty as he did at twenty. He doesn't have to think. It's all been done for him. The script's already written; all the amendments made; lights, camera, action - just follow the word; follow the herd. And if something inexplicable occurs? Well, the Lord moves in mysterious ways, doesn't He? Just have faith and let that be an end to it. That's the difference between religion and science. Science engages the head; religion engages the heart. The only trouble is - the heart wasn't made for thinking. That's not its function. When we use it to think with, catastrophe often follows. Thinking with the metaphorical heart is a self-absorbed, subjective and inaccurate manner in which to seek knowledge. It leads civilisation down the path to Hell by too readily accepting Heaven.'

Everyone was looking at Leslie as if he was somewhere between madman and Messiah.

'Don't you all see?' he concluded, 'The world of our forefathers, hundreds of years ago, clawed its way out of the Dark Ages only because the Arabs had the precision of mind and the forethought to understand the genius of Antiquity. Books were worth a king's ransom then and they are now, but we've failed to recognise it and I'm afraid, everyone, that the future will pay dearly for our lack of sagacity.'

With this he subsided into his chair and said no more.

'Very impressive!' said Elizabeth after a long pause. 'We really have to find that book. Stefan. I want every government department turned upside down. The manuscript could simply have been misplaced. I want its footprints detected and traced. No excuses. Go.'

Elizabeth dismissed Stefan and turned back to the two men but she addressed Lesley, in particular.

'I'll have the whole city put under the microscope, Consul Woodford,' she assured him. 'We'll find that book, and if you're half as good at thinking as you are orating, we'll make some great strides in the next six years. Your thoughts on religious doctrine interest me greatly. We must speak upon the matter later in more detail.'

The meeting ended soon after. It was decided that the nuts-and-bolts stuff of government could wait until later in the week. Nicholas and Leslie were about to enter the elevator when Elizabeth stopped Leslie.

'Go on, consul,' she said to Nicholas, 'I wish to speak with Consul Woodford.'

With a wave and the close of two elevator doors, he was gone.

Elizabeth took Leslie by the shoulder, manoeuvred him to the corner of the room and spoke quietly.

'Consul, I assume that in spite of the lost manuscript you already have some ideas and blueprints of your own? At least I think that's what you started to say to me at the party the other night, but we didn't get much chance to speak.'

'Yes,' Leslie replied, and feeling that honesty was winning him the day he added, 'I couldn't get near you for all of those young, oversexed suitors.'

For a moment Leslie felt that he had overplayed his cards because Elizabeth looked back at him in silence with a startled expression upon her pretty face. But the sun soon broke through the clouds and he watched with delight as a vast smile lighted up her glorious face and a hearty laugh forced its way through those inviting, red lips. She gripped his shoulder more tightly with camaraderie.

'Oh, Consul Woodford,' she laughed, 'what a surprise packet you've turned out to be. An honest politician – now there's an oxymoron.'

Leslie let down his guard and laughed along with Elizabeth. He found the generosity of her laughter compelling and if he hadn't been in love with her before, he certainly was now.

'The reason I ask,' she continued, still smiling in the aftermath of her laughter, and still clasping him by the shoulder, 'is because there was another young man at that party that I would like you to meet. His name is Damien Hill. He's a businessman of some vision, I think, and I was hoping that manuscript or no manuscript, you two might put your heads together. He's a man who has the means to put some of your ideas into action. What do you say?'

'I'd be happy to meet him,' replied Leslie.

The two parted with a smile and Leslie's feet didn't hit the ground until he was halfway across Hyde Park. There he stopped by the old war memorial, beside which sat a much more recent bust of Jeremiah and this reminded him of his troubles.

Beneath the bust, a plaque read: 'In the pursuit of opportunity for all people.' Sitting beneath it was a small boy with big, dark eyes who looked up dolefully at him. Immediately, the bubbles went out of his effervescence. The boy could have been from a Dickensian workhouse. His clothes were mere rags, ingrained with filth. He was unwashed and his hair was oily and unkempt. He had a small, tattered cap in front of him and he was begging. Leslie reached into his pocket and, with a sad smile, tossed in some coins. The boy returned the smile, grabbed the cap and ran off, lest the man change his mind and steal back the treasure.

Leslie watched the boy disappear across the crowded middle-day park. He watched him shrink into a small, brown dot lost in a mass of other small, brown dots. And it struck him forcefully – Jeremiah's and Dunnett's administration had looked to bring individuals opportunity, but the next century had failed that dream. No matter where he looked: north, south, east or west, there were homeless beggars. But there were few people to whom they could beg. The majority of the well-to-do were in the scrapers away from the filthy streets.

As he walked, he ruminated upon this class separation. There were those who were neither homeless, nor wealthy, it was true. There were shopkeepers and salespeople of whatever goods the limited factories of Corporate City could create. There was a basic but sound banking system that employed people and there were many loan sharks. Also, many of the poorer citizens had been employed by the rich. There were attendants of all kinds: tutors and nannies for their children; cleaners for their apartments; tailors for their bodies and hairdressers for their heads. Some women even had handmaidens and many of the elderly rich had all-day carers. These street dwellers, fortunate enough to find employment in this way, lived in the lower levels of the scrapers, mainly for the convenience of the rich. But there were few of them. This was not a robust emerging middle class. The economy was too rudimentary for that. The rich had access to all of the leftovers from the old world. They had a functioning electricity grid. They had food grown by the luckier lower-class members in what fertile ground there was between the periphery of the city and the desolation of the wasteland. They even had alcohol, courtesy of one government brewery and also provided by any street dwellers clever enough to supply it (although this produce was mainly consumed by the employed street dwellers themselves, due to its inferior quality). They were not as wealthy as the tsars of nineteenth century Russia, or the kings of early eighteenth-century France, but they were wealthy enough, especially when compared to the street dwellers who died in droves each winter and who scavenged through the bins of the rich, when they could get away with it. The more Leslie thought about it, the more he marvelled that there hadn't been some major uprising in the past century. There had been riots, some of late, in fact, but never had the poor galvanised themselves into a force to threaten the status quo.

Leslie had spent his entire life in the luxury of the scrapers, thanks to his father, who had been rich. He had been privately tutored and had enjoyed all the trimmings of opulence. In fact, his friends said he was mad to seek public office because it meant a demotion to the lowest levels of the scrapers, just above the street dwellers. But he had insisted and he had achieved his goal. During his young life he had built up a battery of ideas and had always wanted to serve in public office, but until this moment he had never seen so clearly how utterly the present city had failed its citizens. It was no good blaming them, he reasoned, they needed guidance. That was what good government should be about. But he had been so buried in books and ideas that he had not, until now, really considered how to best utilise his ideas to effect government. Technological advance was all very well and he could help provide that, but it must be practical technological advance that served the individual citizens of Corporate City. It must be technology that served Jeremiah's dream. It must be technology shared by all, not only enjoyed by the wealthy.

And then it crystallised. Elizabeth was wiser than she knew. He would get to know this, Damien. He would get to understand how the city functioned and he would tailor his inventions to suit the practical advancement for all. Even if the famously lost manuscript didn't surface, he could still achieve great things for his city. He would join all the little brown dots he was still watching clustering along the streets and join them into a cohesive picture.

And when he had established himself as a scientist and consul of worth - then he would make a pitch for Elizabeth Dawson.

*

EXT.THE MOUNTAINS.DAY

Ramsey's mansion sits silently upon the hill. It is unused and dilapidated.

Two men on horseback ride out of the nearby forest. One soldier wraps a rag around the head of an arrow and lights it.

The soldier shoots the arrow into the dry, old structure and it bursts into flames.

The soldiers ride away.

# Chapter 5

The following Thursday, Elizabeth convened what was officially the first meeting for the triumvirate. So Leslie was amazed to see Damien Hill perched between Elizabeth and Nicholas, sitting patiently behind the polished hardwood table. His amazement was transparent and Elizabeth responded.

'Our friend Damien Hill has graciously agreed to attend today,' she explained with a broad smile. 'He has, unfortunately, resisted my attempt to bring him more permanently into the fold as an adviser, but he has agreed to meet with you today for some preliminary discussions, apropos our conversation the other day, consul.'

Elizabeth awaited Leslie's reply. His natural disposition was to caution. This man was not a part of the body of three who ruled the city and damn it, he was quite good looking and Elizabeth obviously had great regard for him if she had asked him to be adviser. She looked absolutely stunning too in a light green dress. Her beauty was no doubt appreciated by the young businessman she now sat beside. All these thoughts went through his head but he replied courteously, 'Of course,' and seated himself.

'Alright,' Elizabeth began, shaking her dark, meticulously tousled hair in a prelude to her address. 'My second term officially begins today and I intend to make some big waves in Corporate City over the next six years. I need men of vision to accompany me on my journey. That is why Damien is here today. And that is why I am honoured to have been blessed with such capable men as you, Nicholas and you, Leslie.'

Leslie was flattered but Nicholas didn't look all that happy. Damien Hill was impassive.

Elizabeth continued, 'So here is my proposal.

Nicholas and I will oversee the day to day running of government for the foreseeable future. We'll run any new ideas past you, of course Leslie, but essentially, we will embark upon a transformation of the bureaucracy of this city and a cleansing of some troublesome criminal factions whilst you two,' she pointed towards Damien and Leslie, 'will be given full reign to conceive of and execute some more inventive and far-reaching plans.'

Leslie and Damien sat forward in their chairs. Damien's handsome face was radiant with interest. Leslie pushed back his thinning fringe and listened.

'What we need in this city is a firm hand,' Elizabeth stated forcefully. 'The rich would seek to draw us under their spell with promises of gold and reward. The minority groups would woo us with their promises of electoral support and the street dwellers would have us quiver in our boots by rattling their empty scabbards in the streets. But we will not be swayed, consuls. Over the next six years, free of the cancer of election, Nicholas and I will embark upon a radical transformation of the ground conditions in the city while you two visionaries will map out any new inventions that may take us into a wider world. Everything you need will be at your disposal. Whatever machinery and resources you need will be granted. All you have to do is ask and it will be supplied, if humanly possible. What do you say?'

Damien cast a glance towards Leslie, to whom he had never spoken. Leslie didn't return that gaze. Instead, he looked forward, thinking, with his head slightly down, his eyes wide open and his pupils turned upward as if seeking the top eyelashes. It was a picture of deep concern.

'Problem?' enquired Elizabeth.

After a long while Leslie asked, 'Are you trying to squeeze me out?'

'No. No. Of course not,' replied Elizabeth with an expansive waving of her hands. 'Nothing could be further from the truth.'

'Well, it seems like it.'

'How do you figure that?' asked Elizabeth. She appeared to be truly bemused by Leslie's response.

'First of all, I'm the first scientist elected for three decades and when I arrive all the scientific papers have suddenly disappeared. Now I find myself being sidelined with another man, unelected I might add, no offence intended,' he nodded towards Damien who looked back at him without expression, 'and told that the president and the other consul, both of whom represent, and come directly from the higher scrapers, are to make policy in my absence.'

Damien added, 'Excuse me ma'am,' in his pleasant Australian country twang, 'I must admit, he does have a point. It's true I'm not an elected representative.'

Elizabeth replied vehemently, 'That is a ridiculous misconstruction. That is not my intention at all!'

Her stormy outburst stopped all movement at the table. Realising that she had vented rather more of her emotion than she had intended, Elizabeth iterated, much more calmly, 'That was not my intention at all.' She gathered herself in, as if to do so physically was to do so mentally as well. 'What you have to understand,' she continued, now in a measured tone, 'is that voting is not compulsory, so we rely greatly on the votes from the scraper dwellers and those of the growing middle class represented by minority groups. It is they who elect us and ensure at least some measure of consistency in government, inconsistent though I'm sure you think it is right now, Consul Woodford.'

Leslie dropped his head momentarily under the breeze of the rebuke.

'And let me remind you, consul, that the only thing that makes you a scientist, considering there are no such degrees or even universities to award them, is the fact that you obviously have a propensity for invention. Coupled with the fact that I am the serving president and will administer my government as I see fit, I think that it is, to say the least, ungracious of you to tell me that I'm trying to squeeze you out, as you put it, when in fact quite the opposite is the case. I'm offering you the greatest opportunity ever granted to a consul in the last century. I'm offering you unfettered access to government and industrial stores. I'm offering you a chance to put into practice some of those ideas of yours. Word of you has reached me, consul, and also of you, Mr Hill. It is my fervent wish that this city shall rise from its current mire and I have become convinced that you two are the way to achieve that. Nicholas and I can handle the day-to-day machinations. I am freeing you two to forge our city into the future. So please, both of you - do me the courtesy of at least realising when you're being paid a great compliment and granted a great boon.'

Having completed her speech several decibels higher than she had begun it, Elizabeth sat back in her chair and looked back at the others, her head turning swiftly this way and that, awaiting some response. She was wilder than Leslie had ever seen her.

'What do you think, Nick?' Leslie asked, rather bravely, Damien thought, considering the current cloud hanging over the meeting.

Nicholas looked tired and withdrawn. In fact, he didn't look at all well. He was slumped in his chair and he had listened to the exchange with his eyes downcast and doleful.

'I think you should do what President Dawson says,' he replied slowly. 'We can handle things this end.

We won't leave you out of any important decisions, Les. Don't worry.'

'Are you alright?' asked Leslie with some concern. This was not the same vital, hearty man he had met on several occasions before.

'Yes, I'm fine . . . well no actually, I'm not fine really. Everyone always says that don't they, whether they're fine or not?' He coughed. 'I'm not really feeling very well at all,' he said. 'My son, Edgar's had this thing. Perhaps I'm getting it too.' He coughed again.

'Very well,' concluded Elizabeth. 'Obviously, Nicholas is unwell, so there's no point carrying on today. But I'd like you two men to at least have some preliminary discussions today. Leslie? Damien? What do you say?'

They both agreed and soon Elizabeth was gone. Leslie stopped Nicholas on the way out.

'Nick, are you sure you're alright?'

'To be honest, I feel like shit,' he replied. 'I'm afraid I'm coming down with something. His big brown eyes were watery and his podgy face was ruddy, in an unhealthy way.

'Well go and lie down,' said Leslie.

'Right you are, Doctor Les,' Nicholas replied with an attempted smile and he moved stiffly towards the door. But just before he reached it, he turned and said, 'When doors open, walk through 'em, but always take a good look around as you enter the room.'

And he left.

'What did he mean by that?' asked Leslie to himself. But Damien answered.

'I think he means to watch out for me, mate.' Damien slapped Leslie on the back like an old friend. 'Come on, I'll shout you a beer.'

*

The view from Scraper 3 was stunning. The rain had abated and left the sky crisp, clean and clear. Damien and Leslie looked out of the window admiring the surrounding scrapers as a small Asian man with beautifully elegant hands played upon a Steinway in the corner. It was middle afternoon and no one else was about.

'So we're gonna change the world, I hear?' Damien began.

'Apparently,' replied Leslie. 'I wish to hell we had those manuscripts. But yes, I do have some blueprints of my own.'

'Such as?' asked Damien.

'Well, I think we could manufacture a small electric motor that could be attached to scooters and pushbikes that would give our citizens greater mobility. They might even get as far as to the edges of the wasteland and back without recharging.'

This idea twigged with Damien as he thought of his factories. 'Go on.'

'And I've been working on a prototype for a long-range radio utilising the many satellites still circling the Earth, currently without purpose.'

'We could use those?' asked Damien, shifting forward in his seat with interest, suddenly envisioning world trade.

'I don't see why not. There are thousands of them just falling around the planet. We should be able to bounce a signal off at least one of them. Some of them are geocentric, so they're in the same place above the Earth all the time. I might take a few pot shots at one of those. Trial and error.'

'Trial and error?' Damien echoed. 'Mate, if you can really do stuff like that, I'll build whatever you need. We've got metal workshops and welding gear and I know where there's a bunch of mainframe computers in

College Street that haven't been used in a long time - if any of that's any good to you?'

And so the conversation drifted into the afternoon; both men enthusing the other with promises of things to come and all to the background strains of the little Asian pianist.

MONTAGE

Damien and Leslie burning the midnight oil over a table covered in sheets of paper. There are plans and blueprints strewn everywhere. Leslie is animatedly explaining his designs to Damien who is nodding and offering suggestions.

A workman opens a huge roller door. Damien guides an old army truck into a massive warehouse. Leslie watches on as tools and machinery are loaded from the truck. He laughs with satisfaction and pats the equally happy Damien on the back.

Leslie in industrial goggles hard at work shaving steel on a lathe.

Damien searching through old industrial bins and throwing any useful raw material onto the back of a truck.

Elizabeth visiting the men. She is shown a pushbike. Its pedals have been removed and footrests installed. Leslie has attached a small motor to the rear of the vehicle and is demonstrating its speed. Elizabeth beams with pleasure at their progress. She hugs both of them. The two men catch eyes with one another in silent competition.

Damien pulls back a sheet to reveal a huge computer. Leslie is impressed and excited. Damien reveals another and yet another. Leslie shakes his head in wonder. He touches one of the mainframes as if it is a precious jewel.

DISSOLVE

Now the same computers are in full swing flashing and beeping and computing. Leslie points to a map of the world on the wall. He is explaining something to Damien and drawing wavy lines across it. Damien nods as Leslie places three crosses on the map: one above Australia; one above the southern tip of India and one above the U.K.

Leslie sits alone. It is late and the close light of a computer monitor splashes light upon his face. He speaks into a microphone . . .

*

'Come in. Can you read me? Is there anybody out there?'

Leslie was tired. He pushed back his chair from the desk. His face was weary and drawn. The loud sound of white noise filled the darkened room. Leslie rubbed his eyes, moved across the room and turned on the light. Behind him a heavy, old satellite dish was revealed pointing up through a large recently excavated hole in the curved metal roof directly above it. He punched a series of digits into the mainframe and the satellite dish moved a fraction of a degree to the north, almost imperceptibly. He stared at it for a moment, his eyes glazed with fatigue. He wandered slowly down a long corridor towards the men's room, stretching his back and neck as he went.

He rested his forehead upon the wall as he relieved himself into the porcelain. 'Two weeks,' he muttered. 'Two bloody weeks. My head's full of static.'

He was washing his hands when he heard a voice coming from the far room.

'That you, Damien?' he yelled. No response. 'That you, Damien?' Nothing.

Leslie appeared cautiously around the bathroom door. He peered down the corridor and listened. All he could hear was static rasping into the gloom at its far end. He was sure that he had heard a voice, so he looked for a weapon in case of attack. He decided on an old poker that sat in an adjacent room next to a long disused fireplace. Stealthily, he returned into the corridor and, as quietly as he could, crept along it towards the radio room. Slowly, he poked his head around the corner. He could see no-one. The white noise still spewed from the small speakers, but apart from that, nothing.

'Damien?' he repeated, hoarsely. His heart was pounding. He held the poker menacingly in front of him. Crime was rife in this city and he was no hero.

Step by cautious step he entered the room, turning his head this way and that, threatening space with his extended poker.

Then, to his utter amazement, the static noise suddenly ceased and he heard a voice, an English voice, loud and clear through the speakers.

'This is U.K. 1 transmitting via satellite. This is U.K. 1 transmitting via satellite. Come in, please. Come in. We copy you, whoever you are. This is U.K. 1. Can you read me? Over.'

For a second or two Leslie couldn't believe his ears.

He stood with his mouth agape and the poker still menacingly before him. He dropped it and raced to the computer microphone.

'U.K 1,' he spluttered, 'U.K. 1. Hello. Hello. Over.' Leslie held his hand to his head in disbelief and he stared at the stars through the hole above him as he listened.

The voice came again, 'Who is this? Over.'

'This is Leslie Woodford,' he replied. 'From Corporate City. Over.'

'From where? Over.'

'Oh sorry,' stammered Leslie, 'from Sydney. Sydney, Australia.'

There was a moment's silence and for one or two awful seconds Leslie thought that he may have lost the satellite. But not so. The operator opened the microphone at the other end and suddenly Leslie could hear cheers and whoops of delight thundering across the globe. He was startled, until the operator's voice came back to him again, more loudly this time, to keep above the din.

'Sorry, old man! Hold on!' he yelled. 'Keep it down everyone!' and the background party noises quickly diminished. 'Sorry about that,' he explained. He sounded very British. 'But this is our first contact with Australia. Everyone here is very excited. Are there many of you? Over.'

'Several hundred thousand, I think,' Leslie replied. He was in a dream, but he pulled himself together for a pressing question. 'Have you contacted other cities? Over.'

'Twenty-two. You make it twenty-three,' the voice replied, 'but you're the first from the southern hemisphere.'

'Who else do you know of?' asked Leslie. He was beside himself with excitement. He was the first man in Corporate City in well over a century to hear the voice of a foreigner.

'We have Washington, New York and several other cities in the western hemisphere; Baghdad, Teheran and a few more cities in the Middle East; some of the major European centres and quite a few across Asia, including Yangon, Beijing and Tokyo. Welcome to the world. Over.'

Leslie was choked up. He had tears rolling down his face. He was besotted with the love of discovery and the greatness of revelation. He yelled out with delight, but he didn't open the microphone to let London hear his joy.

'Where do we go from here? Over.' he asked when he recomposed himself enough to speak again. There was a quiver in his voice and his stomach felt like someone had been wrenching it from the inside and was trying to get out.

'Sit tight. Remember the frequency. My name is Sidney. Ironic, yes? We have only recently been able to activate the M61 satellite above Australia and we're relaying from M65 above Jo'berg, but that's in motion, so we only have a window of one hour at this time each day. It's three in the afternoon now, so it would be about midnight there. You can contact us each day between about 11pm and midnight your time. Unfortunately, we only have a few seconds transmission left now. But we shall speak again tomorrow. If you have a honcho there get them to the microphone then. Over.'

'Will do,' Leslie replied. 'But tell me, before you go - what are the conditions in the other world cities. Over.'

There was a brief flicker of hesitation before the voice returned. 'It varies. Let's just say that some are coping while others are, well, in some trouble.'

The voice began to crackle and fade. 'Tomorrow. Over and out.' And the white noise returned.

Leslie slumped back into his chair with the most extreme sensation of satisfaction he had ever known. He felt like Columbus discovering the New World, or Newton when he saw the apple fall. He couldn't believe it. He actually pinched his arm to check that he was not asleep. He overdid it a bit and bruised himself and every time he rubbed his arm for the next few days, he thought himself pretty stupid for that.

'My God,' he muttered. He stared up, wide eyed at the stars. More tears erupted from him and he stood and punched the air with glee. Yes!' he roared and his voice rolled beneath the curved metal surface hanging above him.

*

The next twenty-four hours were, without question, the most delightfully excruciating of Leslie's life. He decided not to tell the others of his discovery until they could hear it directly for themselves. He wanted to maximise the impact.

Just after ten forty-five in the evening, Leslie welcomed Elizabeth and Damien into his radio room. The weather was kind again, and when the two entered, the stars were still smiling down on the opening in Leslie's makeshift observatory roof.

'Where is Nicholas?' asked Leslie, as he took Elizabeth's full-length coat, revealing her shapely form in a red evening dress.

'He's still very ill, unfortunately,' she replied sadly. 'The doctors can't seem to work out what's the matter with him.'

'They're calling it a virus,' added Damien, placing his jacket on a nearby chair. 'Then again, that's what they call everything they can't figure out, isn't it?'

'A virus?' Leslie echoed with disappointment. 'You mean he's still sick after, what is it, nearly a month?'

'Yes,' replied Elizabeth, with a slight shake of her

head. 'Ridiculous, isn't it? His son's ill too. The doctors think Nicholas may have caught it from him.'

'I'm really sorry to hear that. I must see him soon. I've been so busy, I didn't even know.' Then, remembering his manners he said, 'Oh please, come, sit.'

The three of them sat in the austere room in front of the computer. Leslie produced a plate of small goods, some cheese and a bottle of champagne.

'I see you've spared no expense on the décor,' said Elizabeth with a smile, as she surveyed the Spartan room. 'We must be celebrating something?'

'We'd better be bloody celebrating something,' added Damien, taking a flute which Leslie began filling. 'Otherwise what the bloody hell are we doing in this old place at this time of night?'

Leslie and Damien shared a smile. Damien knew Leslie well by now. He had a strong sense that Les had had a breakthrough of some kind. Leslie was generally reserved but when something ignited his passion he became as excited as a schoolboy on a cinema date. Damien could see that Leslie was excited now. He was barely able to contain himself. He spilled some champagne whilst pouring, he had a nervous edge to his voice and he was speaking quickly.

'Yes, as a matter of fact I do have a little surprise for you both,' he said with a sing song 'I know something you don't know' tone to his voice. He sat back and sipped his champagne.

'Well?' asked Elizabeth after some time of watching him sip champagne. She was intrigued. 'Are you going to tell us?'

'What time is it?' Leslie asked casually.

'What time is it?' parroted Damien. 'What's that got to do with anything?'

'It's got everything to do with anything,' Leslie replied cryptically.

'Sorry, you've lost me,' Damien replied. 'It's two or three minutes to eleven. And past my bedtime.'

'Mine too,' said Elizabeth, trying to guess the reason for Leslie's obvious excitement. She looked up through the porthole to the stars and then over at the satellite. Then around the room for any clues. 'I give up,' she said with a smile.

She sipped on her champagne with her achingly sensual blue-green eyes piercing Leslie's soul across the rim of the flute. This was his moment. She would love him for this. This of all things: connection; a wide, wide world; a new age. And he was about to reveal it.

'Lady and gentleman,' he announced loudly, here is to our health, to the health of Corporate City and to the health of all the world cities. Cheers!' He held up his glass in salute and the others followed, looking askance at one another as they did so. Damien was about to say, 'What world cities?' but only got as far as 'What worl . . .' when Leslie opened the throttle on the sound control to his computer and static rasped into the room.

'Do you have to do that?' Damien asked above the minor din. 'It's a tad disconcerting.'

But Elizabeth had stopped sipping her champagne and was watching Leslie closely. She squinted her eyes and tilted her head in silent interrogation.

He returned her stare with the champagne flute still to his mouth and with his other hand resting on a button beneath the microphone on his desk.

A voice invaded the room.

'This is U.K. 1 from London listening for Sydney, Australia. Do you read me Leslie? Over.'

As far as Damien's reaction went, the voice may as well have been a bat suddenly flapping in. He stood up in a chaotic flurry, smashing his champagne glass in the process.

'What the hell!' he bellowed. 'What the hell?'

Elizabeth, by contrast, was carved in stone.

Leslie smirked in triumph as he replied, 'Yes, Sidney. I'm here again. Over.'

'No. No. We're Sydney. We're Sydney. Not him,' whispered Damien, shaking his hands at Leslie so that he could recognise his mistake.

'That's his name,' Leslie whispered back. 'Now shhh.'

Damien didn't know what to do. His eyes were darting about and he had become a bag of worms, uncertain where to squirm to. His heart was beating like 'Achilles Last Stand'. He was a ball of adrenaline.

'Nice to speak with you again, hopefully at more leisure. Do you have your prime minister there? Over.'

'No, but I have our president. Here she is.' Leslie smiled as he handed the microphone to Elizabeth. Timidly, she took it.

'This is Elizabeth Dawson,' she said. 'I am president of Corporate City. Over.'

'Hold on,' replied the voice. And another voice came into the room.'

'Greetings, President Dawson,' it said. It was a male voice, probably from a man of middle years. It was an odd voice; a little high-pitched and a bit raspy, but it was unmistakably British. 'This is Prime Minister Green from London. It is a pleasure to speak with you. Leslie may have told you that you are the first city on-line in the southern hemisphere.'

As Green continued, Elizabeth was incredulous to learn what Leslie had already learned the previous night. Then she asked, 'Of these other twenty-two cities, how many are stable and how many are democracies? Over.'

'It's about fifty-fifty at this stage,' replied Green, 'but I'm afraid that the democracies are faring rather worse over all as far as we can tell. There is civil disobedience in the streets of most democracies. Things are reasonably contained here and in the Eastern seaboard of the U.S.A. and Europe's okay to the north, but alas, where there is choice there is dissent. In Asia, the Middle East and in the Balkans, dictatorships and juntas abound and it must be said they currently appear to be the more stable forms of government. Although, to be fair, no city in the world can probably be said to be truly stable. How are things down there?'

So Elizabeth told him of the general stability in Corporate City but was also honest about the growing unrest in the lower class as the classes divided. She explained the basic system that had been adopted for government. She mentioned also that although Corporate City was a democracy, the growing power of some lobby groups would, in all probability, soon lead to punitive action by her government.

Green and Dawson spoke for the full hour and by the end of it she, Damien, and Leslie had learned that although cities were now in contact with one another, trade was still in its infancy because of the difficulties involved in transporting goods. Most of the democracies sounded like very dangerous places where civil armies jockeyed for control. In the dictatorships too there was the usual bloody revolution every so often but it sounded like some quite big populations, like Beijing, were actually doing reasonably well due to the firm hand of government effectively quelling any disquiet that individuals and their lobby groups might feel.

After an hour of conversation it was organised for Green and Dawson to talk the following night and then at regular intervals beyond. When the final 'Over' was 'Over and out', Elizabeth sat quietly for a moment and simply shook her head in disbelief.

'Well I'll be damned,' she said eventually. This was the closest the two men had come to hearing Elizabeth curse. They looked at one another. Damien, who had regained his composure in the course of the hour, cast a wink and a smile in Leslie's direction. But he lost some of that composure, and his cavalier attitude, when several seconds later Elizabeth grabbed Leslie, hugged him with all her might and planted an absolute scorcher of a kiss right on his lips. In fact, Damien was instantly consumed with jealousy.

'Thank you,' Elizabeth whispered to Leslie. 'You're a bloody genius.' And she kissed him again, smack bang on the lips and this time, to his extreme surprise and delight, Leslie was certain that he felt the faintest touch of tongue.

Needless to say he was in a whirl. He was Biggles in a biplane with its tail shot off. He was in a vertical spin without a parachute. As the warmth of Elizabeth's luscious lips pulled succulently back from his, drawing them ever so slightly away from his face as they retracted, Leslie Woodford, scientist, inventor, consul, was a pile of smoking ash crashed in between the trenches. When he opened his eyes, he found Elizabeth gathering her coat and Damien trying to help her put it on.

'I'll escort you home,' he said as he helped her into the garment. He was trying to regain lost ground but the quest was futile for the moment. He must accept that this round had well and truly gone to his rival.

'No, thank you,' she replied. 'I have much to think about. This changes everything.'

'Can't I help you?' asked Leslie, who had rather hoped for more conversation and adulation after the satellite link.

She approached him and took his hand, 'I think you've done more than enough for one night, consul. Goodnight and thank you again.'

And much to Damien's chagrin and Leslie's delight she kissed him once more, although this time in a less passionate manner.

And she left.

'You prick,' said Damien to Leslie.

'A stiff prick,' replied Leslie.

And the two men looked at one another for a moment before bursting into hilarious laughter. They hugged, and Damien even undertook the familiarity of a kiss on Leslie's cheek. 'You clever prick,' he said. 'Well done.'

'Thank you, sir,' Leslie replied breaking the embrace and moving towards the fridge. 'And I have taken the liberty of purchasing some of the finest alcohol available in Corporate City to celebrate this occasion.'

With a theatrical flourish he opened the door of the fridge to reveal a variety of beverages. 'And since the lady couldn't stay, I say we make it secret men's business.'

That sounded alright to Damien.

Needless to say the next morning very soon became the next afternoon at which time the two comrades arose with thumping brains and a great desire to do nothing.

*

Sebastian Levi, caretaker of the Fisher Library, was finishing his rounds for the day. He had been haunted all morning by a short novel he had read earlier that day. It was a simple but magnificent novel by a twentieth century author called John Steinbeck. It was the simplicity and the elegance of the novel that had haunted him for the past six or seven hours since he had read it. Sebastian had no idea what time it was. He had long since stopped wondering about that. It was, in fact, two fifteen in the morning when Sebastian had first stumbled upon Steinberg's book and three twenty-eight when he had finished it. The time mattered little to Sebastian. But by the time the sun was making its presence felt in the east, Sebastian was wandering, thinking deeply somewhere down in the dim quarters of the lower floors of the library he had been caretaker off for over a dozen years. The book haunted him. How could such a treasure destroy someone's life so? And if he found such a treasure, what would he do?

As he cleared out and dusted yet another stack of old home and garden magazines, his eye was caught by something that didn't fit. Sebastian didn't know precisely why it didn't fit, but he had been caretaker long enough to know that it didn't.

He dived his hand deep into the pile within which it resided and he pulled it out. There it was. It was a green, hardcover book, way out of place here, among the magazines and paperbacks.

So unexpected was the find that he looked about from right to left involuntarily to check that none had seen his discovery. They hadn't. In fact, no one had been down here in the bowels of the old library for years. He looked at the cover. There was no title. He flicked through the pages. It looked mainly technical. He looked around again and quietly began to read the script. At first, he was perplexed and then he realised that this was a lost treasure – a pearl. He laughed at the coincidence, pocketed the manuscript and began to walk the long spiral stairway up through the stories, and stories, of the library above.

Sebastian was almost forty. He was a dark-haired, swarthy looking man who had a permanent five o'clock shadow and who had once been good looking. But the years had ignored Sebastian and any potential he might have had, kindled up there in that sharp mind of his. Instead, he was, if anything, a little hunched for those years. He was not hunched with age or disease, but with despondency. The world had shunned him and pretty well forgotten about him. Now he was a willing recluse, purposefully hidden from the world of men, alone and mainly silent in his silent world. Without parents in his memory, without friends to call upon, without love in his life, he had pursued a quiet life beneath Corporate City sifting through the detritus of a former age. No one visited. Very few borrowed. Few cared about such things as books anymore, even though there was little other kind of entertainment. They still didn't come. Occasionally he would find a stray interested person, but this was seldom. Why?

Sebastian had all the time in the world to consider such questions. The problem, as it appeared to him, was that though there were many books still in existence, these were an eclectic collection that gave no clearly defined path in any one discipline. The great destruction of books, that he suspected probably occurred either during or after the great nuclear war of the twenty first century, had removed the great flow of human knowledge. The consistency was gone. 'Contiguity of written texts *is* civilisation,' he muttered to himself as he pottered about. And that probably explained why there were no universities and places of higher learning; why there were no emerging great artists or scientists. As he saw it, he was living in another Dark Age. The intelligentsia had gone and had not returned. The scraper dwellers organised pleasure; the street dwellers organised survival; there was basic organised business and basic organised government and a noisy bunch of organised lobby groups – but no organised, institutionalised thinking. Everybody was waiting for someone or something to pull the city back into the light.

'So what?' he thought to himself. 'If the city is wretched; if the whole planet is wretched, it's not my concern. There's nothing I can do about it. The city rejected me a long time ago.'

And so he thought and he wandered, as he always did, as he was now, up to his small apartment above the library, muttering incoherent bitterness to himself.

There he cleared his battered spectacles and began to read the small, green book.

*

EXT.MOUNTAIN CLEARING.DAY

A few families are gathered around a campfire. They are dressed in rags and furs.

Out of the nearby woods a cavalry of mounted men suddenly appear.

With rifles and machetes the men, women and children are mercilessly slaughtered.

# Chapter 6

It was a very excited Stefan who burst into Elizabeth's office late afternoon the following day. He wore his perennial, crisply ironed beige suit, but Elizabeth noticed with interest that he had several strands of hair marginally out of place, a definite giveaway that he was truly excited.

'I think . . . I'm pretty sure . . .' he stammered as he sped towards her desk.

'Yes?' she asked.

'We may have. I think we may have . . . In fact, I'm sure we have . . .'

'Have what?'

'Found it!' he boomed.

'The book?' she queried, rising from her seat on the buoyancy of the wave.

Stefan nodded with an agonised grin, unable to speak with excitement.

'Where?' she entreated.

'The old library.'

'Well, where is it? Can I have it?' she asked, leaving her desk and approaching him.

'No, no,' Stefan replied, waving his hands about. '*He's* got it.'

'Who's got it?'

'Sebastian Levi.'

'Who?'

'The caretaker of the library.'

'Why has he got it?'

'I didn't find it. He found it. He found the book. And all the time it was just down the road. To think . . .'

'Alright,' said Elizabeth, gently taking him by the elbow. 'Calm down.'

Stefan clasped the hand upon his elbow in feminine embrace, 'I've tried so hard to find it for you these past weeks and now . . .'

'It's alright,' Elizabeth comforted him. 'It's alright.'

He nodded his head in a prelude to tears. She placed her hand on his for comfort. 'You go and have a nice rest. You deserve it. Just take a deep breath and tell me. Where is he?'

'Waiting for you in the library,' replied Stefan, biting his lower lip with his upper teeth.

'Good work, Stefan. A job well done.'

Stefan closed his eyes and pursed his lips together so that they almost disappeared. Then he nodded to show that he agreed with the praise given him.

Elizabeth raced out of the room and by the time she reached the library several minutes later, Stefan was still shaking, drinking a cup of water unsteadily, while three young office workers listened intently to his dramatic tale.

Elizabeth moved confidently into the dank, musty lobby, where one hundred years before Robert and his friends had been assailed and taken by force to meet Ferret for the first time. Her shoes echoed and clattered on the old stone floor. Eddies of spiralling dust erupted in her wake like mini tornadoes.

'Hello,' she said, quietly at first, and then more loudly, 'Hello!' Her salutation bounced off the unadorned and eerie walls.

In the dimness ahead she saw a figure appear in silhouette. It emerged from the gloom through an internal doorway. It did not speak.

'I'm looking for a Mister Levi,' she stated. She took two paces towards the figure and stopped. Still it did not speak. 'Would that be you, sir?'

'Would that be me?' repeated the figure. 'Not if I had any choice in the matter, but as it turns out, yes, it is me. And you are President Dawson.' Sebastian shifted out into the shaft of light illuminating the central portion of the lobby.

It struck Elizabeth, as she watched the butterfly emerge from the cocoon, that this man had some charisma about him. His voice was educated, quiet and sonorous. When she saw him fully cast in the shifting afternoon sunlight, he could have been a pirate from a romantic novel, or perhaps an errant knave, discarded by society and forced into incarceration in this silent and timeless world.

'I believe that you have something that belongs to me?' she said. She sounded confident but she approached him no closer.

But he moved towards her. 'It is the property of the state, I think.'

'I represent the state,' she replied.

'And what is the state?' he asked her, moving into her personal space.

Uneasy, she stepped back half a pace. 'It is what I represent,' she replied.

'Ah, I see. I see,' he said, nodding his head. 'It really is simple when you look at it like that, isn't it?'

Elizabeth was beginning to feel decidedly uncomfortable. She was wishing that she had brought her retinue with her and not simply burst down Macquarie Street and recklessly entered the domain of this whispering and sinister man.

'You have a book,' she persevered. She raised her chin in defiance of this dark-eyed man who stared penetratingly at her over the rims of his glasses. He was far too close for her comfort.

'I have many,' he replied with a slow smile.

'You have one in particular, I believe,' she returned with a further nervous upturning of her chin.

For a moment there was silence. Elizabeth came close to turning on her heel and exiting the building, with the intention of returning later with an entourage of large men. But just before she did, Sebastian whispered, 'Follow me.'

He disappeared through the doorway from whence he had appeared, leaving Elizabeth indecisive, considering her options and momentarily glued to the floor.

A few seconds later Sebastian's head reappeared in silhouette in the doorway. 'Come along,' he said. 'I shan't bite you.' And again he disappeared.

Elizabeth drew in her breath and followed. Down the spiral stairwell she trailed the man and into the bowels of the library. As she descended, she assessed the folly of her action. The man uttered no more words throughout the long journey down.

Eventually they reached the lowest level of the library. They were now well below ground level and around about the same spot where Rueben had met Weena many years before. Sebastian reached a pile of magazines. He turned suddenly. Elizabeth pulled up quickly in response and her heels skidded. The walls echoed with the sound.

Out of the blue he shot a question at her. 'What is the main perquisite of power do you think, President Dawson?'

'Perquisite?' she asked, trying desperately to keep her equanimity.

'Yes. The main perquisite. The main perk.'

'Oh,' she said, brushing her dark tousled hair away from her emerald eyes in consideration of the question. 'Well, there's the ability to help others, of course.'

Sebastian said nothing.

'And the joy that springs from having a sense of purpose and being able to realise that purpose on a grand scale.'

Sebastian still said nothing.

'And, of course, there is a certain self-satisfaction in achieving goals.' She hesitated, 'And, I can't deny that there's a benefit to one's self and one's family when one achieves great office.'

'Aha,' pronounced Sebastian with enough volume to make Elizabeth flinch. 'Aha! Now we are getting closer to it. *Self*-satisfaction. Satisfaction of the *self*. The joy you speak of is the joy the *self* feels from attaining and maintaining its power.'

'What do you mean?' asked Elizabeth, entirely on her guard by now.

'I mean,' replied Sebastian very quietly and intensely, 'that the driving force of power, the major perquisite of power, the main reason for power is . . . power. Those, like you who have it, Miss Dawson, only barely understand this because you *have* it. It is only when one is *dis*empowered that one sees that anger is the expression of the impotent and the powerless.'

Sebastian's voice had risen ever so slightly in volume and Elizabeth was looking upward towards the safety of the world above through the spiralling dust and the myriad books coating the walls. She began to imagine how quickly she could take off one her of her heels and smash this man in the eye with it, should that become necessary.

Sebastian, however, continued without falter, apparently oblivious to the fear his understated tone and volume was engendering.

'You see, Miss Dawson, I have been thus disempowered. I have been angry and frustrated. I believe that I have ability far beyond my station. I believe that I have been overlooked. I believe . . .'

'Stop!' Elizabeth shouted. The word thundered up the walls and dissipated into the books above. 'I've heard enough. I don't care what you believe. I am president of this city and you have something that belongs to me and

I want it back.' She was asserting herself as the bloated lizard displays the fake armour of its gills.

'Belongs to *you*?' Sebastian echoed, completely undaunted. 'You see. That's my point. You see yourself as the state. You *are* the state. You *are* power and power is a means to its own end.'

'That's quite enough,' she repeated. 'Are you going to give me the book, or not?'

'Oh the book's not here,' he replied. 'It's well hidden.'

'Then why are we here?' she said shakily, giving voice to the realisation of her vulnerability. President or no president, she had no power way down here right at this moment. She stared at the man before her. Silently, she began to slide off her long-heeled shoe.

'There's no need to be frightened,' he said, watching the slow but purposeful retraction of her foot from its casing. 'We're here because I want to show you something. But first, before I do, I want a guarantee from you, as head of the state.'

'What are you talking about?' Elizabeth asked, halting momentarily the removal of her shoe.

'I mean that I have made a great discovery – one that will have great consequences for you, for me, and for others. But,' and he looked at her over the rim of his glasses, 'I will not show you without an iron-clad promise that I shall be included in the bounty that this discovery will generate. You see,' he moved closer to her and she did not budge, 'I have been, as I told you, overlooked by the world. In fact it would be more accurate to say that I have been ostracised by it and this book is my opportunity to deal myself back into the game. What do you say?'

He waited for her response at an obscenely close distance from her face. She could smell his breath, but surprisingly, it was not unpleasant, merely unexpected.

'I could have you ripped apart in the public square for what you have said to me,' she whispered. His face was centimetres from hers. His dark eyes were boring deep into her soul. He was a startling and scary man, but he was exciting too in a strange kind of way. She was oddly aroused by his quiet but manic self-possession.

'And way down here, right now, I could do the same to you, Miss Dawson,' he replied. His face was right next to hers now. He edged gently forward and he kissed her softly on the lips. And to her surprise, she didn't resist.

'Come,' he said. And, in a daze, she followed him down the hallway until they reached the end of it.

Sebastian turned to her with a smile. 'I would never have found it without the map. It took me hours to encrypt it but I eventually managed. It led me to the hiding place of the latch that opened the hidden door. I'm surprised, Miss Dawson, that no-one in one hundred years has thought to find its location.'

'What do you mean?'

'It's all in the blueprints.'

'I don't know what you're talking about.'

'Oh some, come, Miss Dawson – a bright girl like you? You're not going to tell me that you never noticed the map and the riddles? The section had the heading: 'Transference.'

'I have no idea what you mean. I've never bothered to read the green book. It's mainly technical. It means nothing to me.'

'Pity,' Sebastian replied, with a glint in his eye. 'Colin Dunnett's blueprints are exceptional. The man was a genius.'

'What about Dunnett?'

'He's the man responsible for what I am about to show you. He's the man you and I are never going to credit with changing the world. The glory will be ours.'

'Responsible for what? What credit? What glory? What are you talking about?'

'Do I have your promise that you will involve me in all matters related to my discovery?'

'I don't know what your discovery is yet, Mister Levi but I can promise you this: if there is financial gain because of it, you will be duly rewarded.'

'No,' he replied emphatically. 'I want more assurance than that. We are talking about far more than wealth. We are talking about power. Real, naked power.'

He held her momentarily with his glittering eye.

She considered him for a short while. There he stood perched like a parrot on some invisible bar, watching her intently. Was he mad? Perhaps. But perhaps not, too. And if he could deliver only half of what his dramatic ramblings seemed to suggest, then whatever it was, was worth owning, even if she did have to share some of it with this strange, enigma of a man. At length she replied, 'If it aids the state, I promise you a share and an ongoing stake in whatever it is you feel you have discovered. Now what is it?'

He reached beyond the corner of the wall and pressed something. The wall slid back and a bright light filled the hallway. Into this subterranean luminescence he led her.

At first, she thought that he was playing a trick upon her. The room was empty except for two metal chairs upon each of which sat a metal cap attached to the chair by a series of rudimentary wires. It was like something out of an old Boris Karloff movie. She would have dismissed it as child's play had she not also noticed a room above looking down upon the chairs. Through the glass she could see . . . what were they? Computers? Mainframes?

'What's up there?' she asked, tantalised by the basic efficiency of the place. Something about it spoke of real quality and scientific enterprise. It was too bulky and solid to be pretend. The room had a definite presence.

'Shall we?' he said, beckoning her towards a tiny staircase leading up to the higher room.

She had lost her fear. She led the way up the stairs and soon she found herself inside a room full of ancient and dormant computers. In the corner sat a black box, about half the size of an average man. She turned towards Sebastian; a question posed within her eyes.

'He's done it all for us,' he replied. 'All we need is someone to fully understand how the system functions and we're away.'

'Away?' she iterated.

'If you trust me,' he replied, moving up close to her and penetrating her with his dark and dangerous eyes, together we will become the most powerful people the planet has ever imagined.'

'I don't know what this is,' she replied slowly, 'but surely, whatever it is, you overstate your case, Mr . . .'

He leaned forward and kissed her on the mouth again - this time with a great deal more passion. Again, she surprised herself by not only acquiescing, but by actually responding, momentarily, to his inappropriate advances.

She pulled away. 'Get the book,' she replied, drawing in her breath unevenly, 'and we will see.'

Sebastian stared at her long and hard and without taking his eyes from her dark, olive beauty, he reached out, placed his hand behind the black box beside him and produced a small bundle of paper. He handed it to her. 'Here is the relevant section. I have the rest of your little green book safely tucked away,' he said quietly. 'Send your finest mind to me. Once they have understood the mathematics and unleashed the physics of this contraption, together, you and I will reinvent this world.'

Elizabeth took the small bundle. She thumbed through it. But as she did, Sebastian thrust his hand forward and stopped her progress. She looked up; startled.

'This is the page you want, my dear,' he whispered.

She looked down and saw the letters I.Q. sitting innocuously at the head of the page and below this the word: Transference.

'This is the future of world government. This is *our* future.'

She re-looked at the page and then stared back up, limply, at Sebastian. He moved slowly in towards her lips and he kissed her slowly and with a great slow-burning lust. She kissed him back. She didn't know why. They did not touch otherwise. They were only joined at the lips. It was as if some unknown quantity had hold of her. As if some certain future had captured her. She was driftwood in the growing swell of a river. He sucked back away from her lips as gravity pulls inexorably away at the river's source.

She was spinning. Yesterday she had been the president of the known world. Now she was in charge of one city in a world full of cities and she was being challenged by an insignificant man in the depths of a musty old library and he was making demands of her power. Not only that, but he was kissing her. He was kissing her and she was aroused and responding. It was all so very strange - all so very strange, but all so very enticing and intriguing. This swarthy, mysterious, strange man promised her power beyond all possibility.

And she was kissing him.

# Chapter 7

'I have too much of the artist within me,' Sebastian confided to Leslie's eager face. 'I tend to see the romance of the flower's blooming rather than the chemical process or the physics within. I loathe myself for this shortcoming, you understand, but it is unfortunately rooted deep within my nature.'

Leslie nodded at every word. He had just met Sebastian. Now they were descending the stairwell towards the lowest floor of the library.

'Elizabeth tells me you've made an important discovery,' said Leslie. 'But I don't understand why you need me?'

'I never studied the maths, you see. That was my mistake. The concepts form in my mind but I don't have the numbers to support the structures.'

'Could you not study?' asked Leslie as they reached the bottom floor. 'Anything can be learned, surely?'

Sebastian stopped and turned. 'It is not *what* we learn but *how* we learn it. I could study my entire life away and still I would only see forests. I want to see the trees as well.'

Leslie said nothing. He could shift between both. Perhaps not everybody could.

Sebastian must have read his mind. 'I asked President Dawson to send me her finest mind. If she has, you will have no trouble unravelling the mystery of the black box, Consul Woodford.'

'Black box?'

'Yes. Are you good at spelling?'

'What?'

'You heard me.'

'Why, yes.'

'And you have a written turn of phrase too, I'll bet?'

'Yes,' Leslie confided. He felt like a defendant unsure of where the prosecution was heading.

'You have been blessed. You have been blessed,' Sebastian muttered with a short grin and a wave of his index finger. He turned, laughed and continued to laugh as he resumed his passage down the hallway. He yelled upward over his shoulder as Leslie scurried behind, 'Very few of us see the building blocks of Lego and the soft edges of the creation.'

Leslie followed, perplexed.

Sebastian reached the door towards the end of the hallway where Weena had once led Rueben. He turned back to face Leslie. 'What would you give,' he asked, 'to be what you are, times ten?'

'I don't understand the question,' replied Leslie. He was captivated by this strange and slightly older man who spoke in riddles and who obviously had a great gift of mind.

'You have the paper I gave Miss Dawson?'

'Yes.'

'Well?'

'I only received it just before we met. Elizabeth gave it to me and I was escorted here. I haven't had anything but a cursory glance at it.'

'I see,' Sebastian replied with a nod of his head. 'In that case, I will show you something and explain what I know. Then I will leave you for one hour and return after that time with some food and drink.'

'Food and drink?'

'You have a long and interesting night ahead of you,' replied Sebastian with a sly smile. And he opened the door to the transference chamber.

When Leslie stepped into the chamber, and especially when he looked up at the console room and saw the mainframes, he drew in his breath with anticipation.

One hour later, Sebastian returned with the food. 'So?'

Leslie didn't answer him at first, so immersed was he in his reading. When he did look up it was with the starry eyes of those journeying back to the restraints of physical reality from the limitless reaches of thought.

'So?' repeated Sebastian, scanning Leslie's face for traces of discovery.

The two men sat upon the transference chairs. Leslie had a transference helmet upon his lap which he now raised towards his eyes in silent amazement. He turned it this way and that and looked closely at the wires connected to it.

'This is incredible,' replied Leslie with a clearing of his throat and several blinks of his eyelids. 'Incredible,' he repeated hoarsely.

'So it can be done?' asked Sebastian nodding his head in affirmation of a deed not yet accomplished.

'Yes,' replied Leslie. He raised his puppy dog eyes up to meet Sebastian's denser, more sinister ones. Then he shook away the clouds of mind and focussed upon him. 'But are you sure that you want to?'

'Want to?' repeated Sebastian, almost reeling back in chair, as if he had been struck by the remark. 'Want to? Of course I want to. Consul Woodford, this is the single greatest gift to man since $E=mc2$.'

'Yes,' replied Leslie thoughtfully, 'and look what happened because of that.'

'Electricity changed the world. Technology must be embraced. We must move from the shadows.'

Leslie straightened in his seat. 'Yes. But that was an external convenience. This is penetrating into the plasticity of the human mind.'

'True,' Sebastian conceded, 'but think - what is the major problem in this city today?'

'Inequality?' offered Leslie.

'Precisely,' replied Sebastian, grabbing him lightly by the forearm. 'And if you can make this system work that will disappear, almost overnight.'

'I don't see how,' replied Leslie, his eyes narrowing in puzzlement.

'Come. Come, young man,' Sebastian responded condescendingly, (in truth he was not all that much older than Leslie), 'He who controls the mind, controls the body; he who controls the body controls the animation of the pieces; he who controls that animation of the pieces, controls the game. Don't you see? We can issue intelligence; regulate the pieces; control the game.'

Leslie had become perturbed by the manic widening of Sebastian's eyes. As he had increased in intensity of speech, so too had he tightened his grip on Leslie's arm. At last, Leslie shook it free. 'People are not merely animated pieces,' he stated. 'Have you sought Elizabeth's permission to do this?'

Sebastian slipped slowly into Leslie's personal space and looked over his glasses at him. 'No. But I will.' His presence was dark; ominous. 'And you will have to agree to fire up this console if you ever hope to see the rest of Dunnett's blueprints.'

'That's blackmail.'

'Yes. It is,' replied Sebastian with an annoying grimace. He was so close that Leslie could count his nasal hairs.

'Very well,' replied Leslie, continuing to labour under this short but awkwardly close encounter with Sebastian's face. 'But I know she'll come down straight away when I return to the office.'

Sebastian did not reply but continued to linger at an unacceptably close range to Leslie's nose.

Leslie had not backed away but he did visibly relax his stance when Sebastian finally stepped back away from him.

'Just set it up and leave the rest to me. We're all in this together,' said Sebastian waving his arms in slow motion from the chairs in which they sat and up towards the console room above. 'We have to learn to trust one another, consul.'

Leslie did a small double take. He had always been told never to trust anyone who said, 'Trust me'. But he was as intrigued as Sebastian by the possibility of thought transference and he figured that any misappropriation of power would be dealt with severely by the president. Elizabeth was friendly enough to him, but it was also true that she had a reputation for ferocity when threatened.

So Leslie went about his business in the console room and did not appear until the following morning. He was unshaven and grubby and sitting back in the transference seat when Sebastian returned.

Leslie looked up. His eyes were tired and he had bags beneath them. 'How did you know I was finished?' he asked.

'Surveillance,' replied Sebastian.

Leslie cast his eye quickly around the chamber but he could see nothing.

'So. Is it done?'

Leslie nodded.

'Excellent,' replied Sebastian. The murky depths of his eyes widened momentarily with pleasure.

'But you can't use it yet.'

'Why not?' Sebastian snapped back; his grin blown away.

'Because (a) you don't know if it's safe; (b) you don't have permission, but mainly because (c) the box is empty.'

'Box?'

'The transference box. The black box. It will need I.Q. stored in it before we can use it.'

'How can we do that?'

'It's relatively simple,' replied Leslie uneasily. 'Listen. Don't do anything until you've talked to the president.'

'She'll be here any minute,' replied Sebastian with a calculated smile. 'I took the liberty of calling her when I saw that you were finished. I hope that you don't mind?'

Leslie didn't mind at all. In fact, he was delighted. His great fear was that he would leave and that this odd-ball man would do something rash before Elizabeth could stop him.

Minutes later, two large guards appeared and moved to either side of the transference room door. Elizabeth pushed past them and entered the room. It buzzed with latent electrical current and the console room above was alight with computer thought.

Elizabeth smiled. 'Is it done?' she asked Leslie.

He nodded. She embraced him.

'Excellent,' she said, clasping her hands together in great excitement. Her eyes flashed and her dark hair tossed around her delightful face like soft pillows of cloud blown gently above a sun lighted ocean.

'We must test the device first,' said Leslie.

'Of course. Of course,' she agreed. 'No one is to use this unit without my permission. This entire library is to be locked until further notice.'

'And how and when are we to test it?' asked Sebastian quietly but intensely.

'How and when I say,' replied Elizabeth curtly. 'From now on, no-one comes into this room without my express permission. Is that understood?'

Leslie nodded in assent but Sebastian was rigid.

'That includes you too, Mister Levi.'

'Madam . . .' he began, but she interrupted him. She had regained her authority, courtesy of armed guards.

'I know you've been here for many years, Mister

Levi. Don't give me any speeches. I won't forget my promise. But first we must ensure that this device is safe.'

'May I speak with you alone for a moment, President Dawson?' asked Sebastian.

'Yes, of course,' she replied. 'Leslie, you may leave us.'

This surprised him. 'But is it . . .' he began.

'Don't worry. I'll be quite safe,' she replied with a smile, nodding towards the guards at the door.

And he exited the library leaving the president several floors below with the inscrutable and slightly scary Sebastian Levi.

*

Later that afternoon Leslie knocked on Elizabeth's door.

'Come in!' she shouted back.

'I thought you'd let me know when you got back,' asked Leslie as he entered.

'Do I have to tell you every time I get back?'

'Well, no,' replied Leslie with a stifled and embarrassed laugh.

'What can I do for you, consul?'

'I just wanted to make sure that you were alright and to find out what's happening with the transference unit.'

'Well, as you can see, I'm fine and as for the unit, as I told you, it's off-limits to everyone for a while, until I decide what to do with it.'

'I've been thinking, perhaps we could test it on animals? We don't have to try it on higher order animals. What about rats? They're smart already. Let's catch some and . . .'

'Consul, I'm very busy. So, unless you have something else to discuss, I'll see you at tomorrow night's dinner.'

'Yes, but . . .'

'Good day,' she said abruptly and she cast her eyes back down towards her paperwork.

Leslie was speechless. What had happened? Why was Elizabeth being so curt with him?

Later that evening, over dinner in a restaurant, he asked Damien the same question.

'Don't ask me, mate,' Damien replied after downing a rough glass of ale. 'All I know is that she hasn't noticed me for yonks. I thought I had a show there for a while but I think I'm out of the running. Business only.' And he downed some more ale.

'She's never been like that to me before,' Leslie mused. 'I don't like this Levi bloke.'

'Never trust a librarian,' replied Damien. 'He's been cooped up in there for years. What do you expect? He's a weirdo.'

'Yeah, well he's a weirdo who's getting into the ear of the president. That's what worries me.'

'Touch of the Rasputins,' replied Damien with a rugged smile.

'I'm not joking. And where's the rest of the book he promised me?'

'You'll get it. Don't panic,' said Damien, patting Leslie hard on the back as if he meant to burp him or dislodge some object in his throat. He smiled broadly, 'On a brighter note, mini-scooter production is underway. How are our friends overseas?'

'That's another thing,' replied Leslie pensively. 'What about that? Elizabeth's taken over that too. I went back to my radio room after I talked with her today and the locks have been changed. I called her and asked her about it and she told me that it was all under control, but she didn't give me any specifics. Damien, I think she's cutting us out of the loop.'

'Don't get paranoid. She *is* the president.'

'Am I? Am I being paranoid? Perhaps. But as far as I can see, we keep settin' 'em up and she keeps carrying 'em off. What's she up to?'

Damien sat forward and placed his hand kindly on Leslie's shoulder, he repeated emphatically, 'You're being paranoid. Everything'll be okay.'

Leslie appeared far from convinced.

'It'll be fine,' iterated Damien. 'This is how things are done in Corporate City. Trust me. I've been dealing with these people for a long time. Elizabeth's part of a family that's been running this town, one way or another, for almost a hundred years. These politicians are a weird mob. She'll come good. Just don't worry about it.'

'But I thought she liked me,' replied Leslie with a forlorn moue and in a tone that was either endearing or pathetic, depending upon your bias.

Damien found it endearing. He laughed. 'She does, mate. She does. Look what you've already done for this city.'

'No. I mean *liked* me. You know as in . . .'

'Oh. I see,' nodded Damien in recognition. 'Well, we both thought that I suppose.' He sat back into his chair. 'But it's probably best to separate business from pleasure. Although, she is an absolute spunk.'

Leslie, who was drinking at the time, gagged on his drink in a small gust of laughter, spilling some in the process. 'Where the hell did you hear that expression?' he asked as he mopped some beer from his chin.

'My old man used to say it,' Damien replied with a friendly wink. He sat forward in earnest. 'Listen, don't worry yourself. Just do your job, just like you are now and we'll let the president steer the ship. I don't know why you're worried. She's doing all the tough day-to-day stuff.'

'Whatever happened to you and I being visionaries?'

'We are, mate, we are. Listen, you and I are already revolutionising the transport industry. And that's just the beginning. Solar energy: wind energy – all your good ideas'll come to fruition. Give it time.'

'Yeah, but that book?'

'Mate, with the amount of stuff you've got in that grey matter of yours,' he rapped his knuckles lightly on Leslie's cranium, 'what the hell do you need a book for? Now come on. I'll buy you another beer.'

But as Damien called the waiter, Leslie was deeply concerned. He had set up a console that would be the realisation of Colin Dunnett's dream. If he had been successful in following the instructions given, and he believed he had, then transference of intelligence from individual to individual would be a reality. But he couldn't follow up. He couldn't test the machine. Elizabeth had temporarily banished him. Why was she so changed? And so suddenly? Why was there still no sign of the elusive book? And what was that bloody Sebastian Levi up to?

*

There were more riots in the southern part of the city later that month. Police detained twenty people.

# Chapter 8

Leslie and Damien worked together on various projects over the next month. It had been nearly a fortnight since Leslie had seen Elizabeth and several weeks since he had seen Nicholas. So he decided to pay his fellow consul a visit.

'Hello, sir,' said Edgar politely as he opened the door. 'Please come in?'

'Thanks,' replied Leslie.

He handed his raincoat to the young man. He was struck by his height but also by his gauntness.

'Lost some weight?' he asked as he watched the spindly frame of the teenager hang up his raincoat, wet yet again by the late July rain.

'I've hardly eaten for the last couple of weeks,' he replied.

'That's no good,' said Leslie, like a father. 'You can't go on like that.'

'It's okay. I'm still eating some food, just not much. I'm on a special diet I buy separately.'

'I see,' Leslie replied with a small nod.

'Neither of us have been very well – 'specially Dad,' Edgar replied, 'but I think I actually feel a little better.'

Edgar led Leslie to the bedroom. The aroma of sickness hung strongly in the air even before he reached it. It was a musty, airless pall; an old sodden trench coat thrown upon the room.

'Les,' croaked Nicholas, trying without success to raise himself upon his elbows.

Leslie stopped him, 'Don't get up,' he said and Nicholas willingly obliged.

'Thanks,' he replied, dropping back comfortably into his fluffy pillow. 'I don't seem to have any strength these days.'

'It's been over a month,' said Leslie, as if this had somehow escaped Nicholas.

'Don't I know it,' he replied, coughing and reaching for his bedside water as he said so. Edgar helped him.

'What do you think it is?'

'No idea. And neither have the doctors. God knows I've seen enough of the bastards. How are things at the office?'

'What do they say it is?' Leslie pursued, not put off by Nicholas' bravado. The man looked awful. He had shed multiple kilos to the point where his face, once affably creased with small rivulets in the fat, had now become haggard and worn, like the bountiful banks of a river after a prolonged period of drought. He looked dry. He looked unwell and frail. And he smelled sick.

'Oh, they don't know. They don't know. Hopefully, it's not cancer or something terminal. He laughed weakly, as if to make a joke of it all, but Leslie was anything but amused.

'Who's your doctor?'

'Mate,' replied Nicholas, 'you're making too much of this. It's a bloody virus, that's all. Now tell me – what's going on back at the factory?'

So Leslie told Nicholas of all that had happened, including his misgivings about Elizabeth's behaviour. Nicholas nodded thoughtfully throughout and he sighed deeply when at last the information was imparted.

'I'd heard about the radio contact. Fantastic. Well done,' he said clasping Leslie's forearm weakly. 'And as for Elizabeth, well, I'm not surprised. She's a fickle one. I told you not to mix pleasure with business.' He coughed riotously for some time, arching his body upward from the bed in convulsion, before finally slumping back into his pillow. 'But I hadn't heard about the transference thing.'

'Perhaps I should let you sleep,' offered Leslie who

had become aware of Edgar's eye contact across the bed.

'Yeah, come on, Dad. You should get some rest,' Edgar recommended.

Nicholas was too weak to even protest. He looked like he was half asleep already.

Edgar led Leslie out of the room and towards the door.

'Has he been like this the whole time?' asked Leslie, forlorn furrows lining his high brow.

Edgar nodded, 'He's falling away. He's not getting better. Can you speak to someone?'

'I'll see what I can do, son,' he replied warmly. 'Don't worry. He'll come good.'

But as Leslie stepped from the scraper apartment and looked out sadly upon the rain pelting down upon the window at the end of the corridor, he was a long way from actually believing that.

He approached the window and stood for a few minutes, staring as the wind drove the relentless rain in gusts upon it. He listened to the machine gun bursts upon the glass and he watched as his own reflection was refracted by the smears and chaotic flows. He saw his high forehead refracted unevenly in the glass and he watched as the mini tsunamis swept across the landscape of his large brown eyes. And he thought of Eliot's 'Prufrock', which his father had read to him when he was a child. And he made a resolution.

Several minutes later, in his saturated raincoat, he was sweeping past Stefan and advancing upon the president's office.

'Hey. You can't go in. The president's in a meeting!' bleated Stefan.

Leslie thrust open the door.

He found Elizabeth in the full embrace of Sebastian Levi. They broke their kiss abruptly as he entered.

'What in God's name . . .' he stammered.

'Haven't you heard of knocking, boy,' snapped Sebastian.

Elizabeth adjusted her dishevelled hair and grabbed for a tissue to clean up her lipstick. 'You shouldn't come barging in like that,' she chided Leslie. Then she turned towards him, adjusting her dress.

'You and *him*?' He pointed an accusatory finger at Sebastian.

'Why not me?' Sebastian fired back. 'Or perhaps you think she should prefer you, you balding little egghead. Look at you. You're all wet.'

Leslie's eyes widened with anger. But even as his senses went into overdrive, he noticed something strange about Sebastian. He was standing taller; he was clean shaven and he was dressed in a suit. Gone was the defeated ambience of his former self. He appeared to be strong, confident and self-possessed.

'What happened to you?' asked Leslie, his rage suddenly subdued.

'Nothing happened to him,' replied Elizabeth. 'Now please, go.'

Leslie turned his eyes back to her. 'Is this the face of gratitude?' he asked her. 'Is this my repayment for all the work I've done for you?'

'You've provided the groundwork, yes,' she replied, 'but for the moment I don't need your services.'

'That's all very well,' countered Leslie, 'now that you're underway you've cut me adrift. I want to be a part of it, Elizabeth. I want to talk with other cities and be able to help *this* city. I want to be part of the solution. I want to help restore order and equality to the people of Corporate City.'

'You want to fuck Elizabeth,' replied Sebastian with a sneer.

'Ssh,' said Elizabeth, quietly into his ear. 'Don't, Sebastian.'

'I beg your pardon?' replied Leslie with his mouth hanging pendulously open.

'You heard me, boy. Don't give me your claptrap. I know what you do your thinking with. Now go back to your little motor-scooters or whatever they are and let us get about the business of controlling this city.'

'Us? Controlling?' echoed Leslie. 'Elizabeth, what is he talking about?'

But Elizabeth had turned her face towards the rain pelting onto the window and would say no more.

'Elizabeth?'

She would not answer.

'Go away,' muttered Sebastian, also turning his back upon Leslie and wrapping his arm around Elizabeth, as if Leslie had been the offending party.

Leslie couldn't believe what he was seeing. He wanted to speak, but no words would come. He had been used. He stared at the floor as if the answer was somehow there but all he found was a carpet wet with the water issuing from his raincoat. He looked again towards the backs of Sebastian and Elizabeth and beyond them to the cascading waterfalls pouring down the window of the scraper. It was nothing compared to the tears that he felt welling within him. He turned, pushed past Stefan in the doorway, and left.

Stefan watched him pass and then returned his amazed gaze towards the portrait of love framed by the large window. There was his boss, the president, her head resting upon the shoulder of the librarian. He had his arm around her shoulder, gently stroking her hair. He was obviously comforting her and, just as obviously, she was asking for that comfort. Stefan went to speak, then thought better of it. Quietly, he closed the door.

On the far side of it he stood for long time, unravelling threads and unwrapping parcels of the past few weeks within his mind. Suddenly, he stepped away from the door, grabbed for his umbrella and followed the water trail Leslie had left behind.

Soon he found himself outside of Leslie's office, hanging his brolly on a hook.

'Oh, hello,' said Mark with a smile. Then seeing Stefan's expression he added, 'Is everything alright?'

Leslie came out of his office.

'I wonder if I could have a word with you, consul?' asked Stefan.

Leslie nodded and motioned that Stefan should enter. Mark looked up hopefully and was rewarded by another nod. He grabbed his Dictaphone and followed.

Leslie was in no mood to talk. He stood quietly beside the window as Stefan and Mark sat beside each other on the far side of his desk.

Mark clicked on his Dictaphone but Stefan placed his hand upon Mark's. 'Do you mind not taping?' he asked.

Mark nodded chivalrously and turned off the recording device.

'I hope I'm doing the right thing coming to you,' he said, biting his lip and raising his eyes. 'You see, my loyalty is with the state before it is with any representative *of* the state. I've seen several administrations and . . .'

Leslie held up his hand to assure Stefan that he understood, but he did not turn his eyes away from the window.

Mark patted Stefan's hand for reassurance.

Stefan smiled weakly, 'When I saw the president today with Mr Levi and especially when I heard him include himself in a position of authority, which I'm sorry, is untenable . . .,' he faltered, 'it made sense of a few things I've noticed over the past couple of weeks - something that's now worrying me.'

Leslie's ears pricked up. He dropped his chin down and to the left as he listened.

'In particular, it was something that I overheard a few nights ago. I was over at your radio room, Consul Woodford. I'd taken the president over there, as requested. It was a matter of state security, she had said, and so I stayed in the car and she went in alone. But shortly after she left the car, I noticed that she'd left a folder on the back seat . . .'

FLASHBACK

EXT.STAFF CAR.NIGHT

Stefan sits alone in the car.

INT.STAFF CAR.NIGHT

He notices the folder lying on the back seat. He grabs it and exits the car.

EXT.LESLIE'S WORKPLACE.NIGHT

Stefan slips through the gate and up into an external stairwell.

INT.LESLIE'S CORRIDOR.NIGHT

Stefan enters the corridor. He sees a light at the far end.

He approaches the light. As he does, he hears voices and

a burst of radio static coming from the room.

He is about to enter but he hears a male voice and stops just outside.

DISSOLVE

'I stopped because I knew from some other things I'd overheard that whatever the president was doing in your radio room, consul, was top secret. So I, of course assumed that the president would be alone, or perhaps that you, or even Mr Hill might be present, but the voice I heard was neither of you. So I listened by the door . . .'

FLASHBACK

INT.LESLIE'S CORRIDOR.NIGHT

Stefan listens as a male voice speaks on the far side of the door.

SEBASTIAN(OFF)
We can work together on this, gentlemen. This is the biggest prime mover for social change since the Communist Manifesto.

Stefan presses his ear to the door but the reply on the radio set is muffled and indistinguishable.

SEBASTIAN(OFF)
If you doubt the veracity of my statements, prime minister, I suggest you challenge me to

a test. I'm telling you it works! And make no mistake, all of you city representatives tuning in tonight, if you pay for the rights, you'll not only dominate your cities but you'll also find ample trade in other cities who adopt this system. I will see to that.

Stefan decides against knocking on the door and quietly withdraws back down the corridor.

INT.STAFF CAR.NIGHT

Stefan looks back up at the building to make sure no one is coming. He opens the folder Elizabeth has left behind.

Inside the folder is a green book. Stefan flashes through it. He looks up from the pages in realisation.

DISSOLVE

'I realised that this was the green book we'd only recently recovered from the library, but I couldn't make sense of the radio conversation. I didn't recognise the male voice at the time, but I now realise of course that it was Mister Levi. I was confused. Of course, I said nothing to President Dawson when she re-entered the car. I looked in the rear-view vision mirror at her a few times during the journey and I'm sure that she'd been crying.'

Leslie nodded as pieces of puzzle dropped into place. But Stefan and Mark, who knew nothing of transference chambers and radio contact with far away cities, could only guess at the meaning.

'So she has the entire book now, does she?' he muttered to himself. Then back to Stefan he asked, 'Anything else?' He was still facing the window so as not to show his growing anger.

'Just one more thing,' Stefan replied. 'Last night I came back late to pick up some things and I heard an argument in the president's office.'

FLASHBACK

INT.OUTSIDE THE PRESIDENT'S OFFICE.LATE

Stefan is gathering some papers from his desk when he hears raised voices coming from the president's office.

He moves towards the door.

> ELIZABETH (OFF)
> And I want you to stop! Please stop! Oh, I don't know what to think any more. Why isn't it helping?

> SEBASTIAN(OFF)
> Give it time. Give it time. Don't you see? They will come to us.

> ELIZABETH (OFF)
> That's not what I mean. It's not as clear . . . Oh, I don't know what I mean.

> SEBASTIAN(OFF)
> It will all make sense in the end, Elizabeth. Trust me.

Stefan grits his teeth, knocks loudly and pushes through the door.

## INT.THE PRESIDENT'S OFFICE.NIGHT

Elizabeth composes herself. She turns to face Stefan as he forces his way through the door.

In the background, Sebastian has his face away from Stefan, towards the window.

                    ELIZABETH
        Stefan? What can I do for you?

                    STEFAN
        I heard voices, Miss Dawson, and I was
        making sure that you were alright.

Stefan casts a glance towards Sebastian's back.
                    ELIZABETH
        Yes. I'm fine, Stefan. Mind you take your
        brolly now. It's still raining.

                    SEBASTIAN
        Yes, President Dawson.

Stefan bows politely and withdraws from the room.

On its far side he looks concerned, before leaving the darkened room.

                    DISSOLVE

'Which brings us to tonight,' Stefan concluded with a large sigh. He looked up to Leslie for advice.

'Gentlemen,' Leslie said, after a long silence. 'There is an old Chinese curse which says, 'May you live in interesting times.' Well, I'm afraid we're about to.'

# Chapter 9

It was as Leslie had feared. Elizabeth refused to take any of his calls or requests for a meeting. She also refused to remove the guards posted outside both the library and his radio room, or to give him a pass to enter either. He was unable to resume experiments on the transference machine or contact with the far away cities with which he, he kept reminding himself, had made contact possible in the first place. She had cut him completely out of the picture. It seemed that his sole contribution to the advancement of Corporate City was to be the motorised scooter.

'And I'm telling you,' Damien replied to Leslie's suggestion that they break into his radio room, 'if you do that, you're on your own, mate. I may be your friend but I also value my life.'

'What's that supposed to mean?'

'It means, old chum, that at the moment you and me are on the right side of the law. And we're doing alright. Pretty soon those scooters will roll on out and we'll be famous. Okay, so the president's cut you out. So what? She's the president, for God's sake. The president always has the final word. But let me remind you of those rioters from a couple of months ago. They were all executed as criminals of the state. So keep your head down, or you might get it chopped off.'

'Elizabeth wouldn't do that to me.' Leslie was staggered at the thought.

'Maybe, maybe not, but she didn't hesitate to use your services and then piss you off, did she?'

'I'm certain that she wouldn't have me killed. If I'm any judge of character . . .'

'Well obviously you're not,' Damien interrupted, 'because until a couple of days ago you thought that the sun shone out of her arse and that she was in love with you.'

'I'm sure there was something there. I'm sure there was.'

'Les, I love ya, mate, but I've gotta be honest, you're like the bloke who goes to a strip joint and thinks the stripper's coming on to 'im. Once you've paid your money, she's on to the next guy.'

'That's an ugly analogy.'

'True,' admitted Damien, 'but it fits, doesn't it? Look, she flirted with you, she flirted with me, now she's flirting with what's 'is face, the librarian. I've known her family for a long time, mate, and I'm telling you – this may be a democracy in name, but the executive power is usually in the hands of about six families in this city. They're a law unto themselves. Elizabeth'll play one off against the other until she gets what she wants. She's a politician, mate, and a successful one at that. Don't cross her, or you'll regret it.'

This made Leslie reflective. 'That's what Nick said too.'

'Oh yeah? How is he by the way?' asked Damien, glad to be off such a thorny subject.

'Still sick,' replied Leslie. 'I'm going to see him after this.'

'Give him my regards.'

An hour later Leslie did so, but Nicholas was in no fit state to reply. His meal sat, untouched, on a tray in front of him. He lay back with his eyes shut.

Leslie sat at the end of Nicholas' bed staring at him, squinting with thought. He moved beside him and closely examined his fingernails. Then he felt the skin around his jowls. A puzzled expression crossed his face. He plucked a hair from his head but the sick man was so out to it that he didn't even flinch. Leslie found a plastic glove by the bedside and gently placed the hair sample into it.

He stared intently at Nicholas from close up for some time but the patient did not stir. Then Leslie looked at the dinner plate. It was a seafood dish of some kind and it was prepared elegantly.

'Edgar!' Leslie shouted and soon Edgar's face appeared at the door. 'Did you make this food for your father?'

'No,' replied Edgar, 'that came from Macquarie Street, courtesy of the government.'

'Are you eating this stuff?'

'No. Remember? I told you. I'm on my own diet.'

'That's right,' replied Leslie, pensively. Then, moved by a sudden impulse, he took a chunk of crab meat from the plate and pocketed a small, sealed bottle of drinking water. 'I don't think your father will miss this,' he said. And he left.

Three hours later, he returned. He appeared to be angry. He stormed past Edgar, who had opened the door for him, and he blustered his way quickly towards Nicholas' room.

Edgar followed. 'Is everything alright?' he asked as he entered the room, where he was amazed to find Leslie's bottom in the air and his head searching under his father's sick bed. He soon emerged with a test tube filled with urine.

'Can you cook?' he asked Edgar.

'Not really,' stammered the boy, 'Dad usually . . .'

'It's time to start. Your father is not to eat any more of this prepared food. Throw it away, but, if anyone asks, tell them he's eating it. Do you understand?'

Edgar nodded. 'Yes, but . . .'

'No questions. Not yet. Just do it.' He foraged in his pockets with his free hand. 'Here. Give these to your father whenever he'll take them.'

'What are they?'

'Charcoal tablets. If you can get him to eat some

burned toast that will help too.'

'I don't understand.'

Leslie took the young man by both shoulders. 'Edgar, you must trust me. Do you?'

Edgar nodded.

'Good, then pack two suitcases: one for yourself and one for your father.'

'We don't have any suitcases,' replied Edgar, somewhat bewildered. 'Les, there's nowhere to go. Is there?'

'Son,' said Leslie sadly, 'just do it.' He left hurriedly.

Edgar stood, staring at the door for some time after Leslie had passed through it. The whole encounter had been so rapid and strange that he gave his head a quick short, sharp shake to convince himself that he hadn't imagined the whole thing.

*

Back at home in his apartment, Leslie had assembled a small makeshift lab and was examining Nicholas' urine sample, when he heard the same voice he had heard a thousand times before but had never actually listened to. It was that of a wretched man with a red beard who made a nuisance of himself by standing on soap boxes all around the city. He was a well-known stirrer. He must have been thrown into gaol at regular intervals because every so often he would disappear for a period of time and then reappear, bellowing out as vociferously as ever. Leslie tossed him a few coins occasionally. The man appeared to have a wife and young child. Whenever Leslie threw money into the hat the woman would quickly scramble to protect the charity. But although Leslie had always professed to be a man of the people, he had to confess he had never really felt any compassion for the man and his family and he had certainly never really listened to the message he was espousing – until now.

On this particular evening, the man had chosen below Leslie's window to trumpet his anti-government message. Leslie stood quietly above on his balcony, listening.

'Class struggle is the basis of all human relations!' the large, bedraggled man was hollering. 'We have nothing but our labour to sell! We have no means of production, and we are kept from the reins of government by the ruling class who perpetuate our poverty as a means of controlling us!' On he rattled, to a largely empty street, for it had started to rain again and most of the city street-dwellers were seeking whatever protection they could from the harsh late July night, huddled around bins alight with whatever scraper-dweller flammable throw-a-ways they could find. Flat against the wall behind the shouting man, bravely protecting a child from the ever-increasing rain was a woman, bundled up in filthy grey rags.

Leslie bit his lip with indecision, but eventually nodded like a samurai to some invisible shogun and minutes later the filthy man, woman and child were in his lounge room shivering beside the small heater.

The man, whose hair was shoulder-length and matted beyond redemption, eyed his host with great suspicion. Leslie handed him a bowl of meat and motioned that they should eat.

'There's no need for sign language,' stated the man, gruffly, as he handed the bowl to his wife. 'I can understand English.'

'Sorry,' replied Leslie. 'I feel as awkward about this as you do.'

'I don't feel awkward,' said the man.

'You don't?'

'No. I'm just wondering why the hell you brought

us up here?'

'That stuff you're always shouting about. That's Marxism, isn't it?'

'What of it?' asked the large man through a mouth full of minced meat.

'How did you come to know that?'

The man stopped chewing. He looked Leslie up and down. 'Are you the police?'

'No,' replied Leslie. 'I'm one of the two newly elected consuls and I'm interested in your thoughts.'

'Why?'

'I want to change the way we live in this city. I want more social equality. I want to understand the needs of the poor.'

The man erupted with laughter at this. 'Do you now? Well, let me tell you something, my fine *richly* feathered friend - what the poor need are the basics of life and some sort of opportunity to raise themselves out of the gutter. If you can give us sanitation and access to doctors, that'd be a start.' He cast his eye around the room. 'But it's tough, isn't it, sir, to inveigle your economy with lesser economies? It's hard to be munificent when your island is bountiful and those surrounding are poorly stocked. It means that you soothe your wretched moral conscience at a cost. You might have to give up some of your finery to achieve your objective.' He scoffed some more meat before returning the bowl to his mud-besmirched woman, who would not have been out of place as a human in the original version of the 'Planet of the Apes'.

Leslie's eyes were drawn momentarily to the woman's breast and to the tiny child suckling there. Pity pierced him. 'I want to help,' he said quietly.

The man squinted at Leslie, as if trying to gauge his mettle, then relaxed the tension in his face as if he had made some decision. 'Alright,' he said, after downing a glass of water, 'I wasn't always living in the streets. I used to live in the scrapers. I was born into wealth, but I chose to give that up when I realised that I was living a lie – as you are now.'

'Living a lie?' replied Leslie, incredulous. 'I'm not living a lie. I'm trying to help. And I'm not sure that I believe your story anyway. No one would leave the comfort of the scrapers for the poverty of the streets.'

'I did,' replied the man simply. 'And you *are* living a lie.'

Leslie was becoming annoyed. He had invited this man into his home. The dishevelled fellow was all wet and stinking and here he was ungratefully telling him that he, a consul, didn't care about the welfare of people in Corporate City. The nerve of the man.

But the man hadn't finished.

'Let me tell you something, sir. We don't know each other's name and neither of us need to. You're rich and I'm poor and that's the way the world goes – unless – those in power think about those they govern, rather than themselves. Public office should be a burden freely endured, not an invitation to the riches of the pigs' trough. My whole adult life I've strained to be heard over the clinking of champagne glasses. And, quite frankly, consul, I'm sick of it.'

Throughout the man's tirade Leslie had watched him. He was ursine; a bear of a man; almost Viking-like with his massive red beard, long straggly hair and all wrapped in Hessian rags. Leslie was struck by the man's passion, by his conviction and also by his eloquence. He had been well educated, certainly, so it was probably true that he had once been a scraper-dweller. And hadn't he, himself, chosen to live in the lower levels of the scrapers to achieve public office? And wasn't what the man was espousing precisely what he himself believed? He stormed his thoughts to a climax and blurted, 'I'm going to break the law. There's probably corruption occurring in high places and I want to stop it. I'm going to commit treason and I want you to help me. Everyone else I know has too much to lose.'

The admission was electric. Leslie stopped. He couldn't believe what he had just said. But there it was. He had said it. It couldn't be unsaid. He watched carefully as the stunned man stared back at him. His wife also looked at him with clear, intelligent eyes, then they looked, one to the other, and back to him. Pinter's counterfeit silence hung heavy on the room for some time.

'Will you help me?' asked Leslie, his words cutting through the haze of his admission.

The man hesitated. He looked to his wife and child again. 'It sounds dangerous,' he replied, no longer full of fire and vitriol but subdued like a teenager, suddenly in realisation of the ramifications of his actions.

'Well of course it's bloody dangerous!' Leslie blasted back. Having related a huge state secret, albeit one he could deny if it ever came to that, he was now infuriated by this man's sudden recalcitrance. 'You're not going to tell me that you're going to back down, now that a concrete proposal's been put to you?'

The man said nothing but looked again to his wife and more particularly at his child.

'Listen,' Leslie continued, having seen the man's glances towards his family, 'I understand that you have a family. I don't, okay? I have no family to consider. I can see that you do, but - here is a chance for you to help in a practical way. Here's a chance for you to make a real contribution. Rather than yelling about it you can do something. I'm offering you a chance to act. And I promise you I'll do everything to help you if something goes wrong. What do you say?'

The red bearded man looked like a prize fighter

who had just taken a slug unlike any other he had ever taken before. He appeared momentarily groggy and disoriented. Fantasy had become reality and he was uncertain whether he was equal to it. Eventually her stammered - 'Okay.'

'Good,' replied Leslie. 'Your wife and child are welcome to stay here for the time being, so long as they don't touch any of my equipment. There's food in the fridge. I'm Leslie.' He held out his hand.

The Viking man stood straight and tall as if remembering, 'I'm Johannes,' he said.

*

This time it was the corpse of a small boy that sat slumped in the chair. The metal helmet was still attached to his head and his limbs were splayed this way and that in death's contortion. His right elbow had actually snapped with the vigour of his final spasm. Sebastian held the arm by the forearm and jiggled the lower part of the arm as if he was weighing ingredients for a meal.

'I must clamp them down in future,' he said to himself. He unhooked the dead boy from the headpiece and cast him away from the chair. He landed like a discarded rag doll, his limbs askew and his face, in one final indignity, came to rest at the arse end of an old woman, also in rags and also dead. She, in her turn, had been deposited upon a middle-aged man, and he, upon another. In all, the boy joined seven corpses piled up like a bonfire in the corner.

'Clear the room!' screamed Sebastian through his thin gauze mask. To himself he muttered, 'I must find a quicker mode of disposal.'

Two hulking guards entered. They appeared to be witless thugs, incapable of dissent. Obediently, they grabbed two corpses apiece and dragged them from the room. Sebastian removed his mask and climbed the stairs to the transference console while the bovine attendants continued their gruesome cartage.

He cast his stormy eyes towards the black box which sat beside a mainframe in the corner of the room. He read its display and he grinned with pleasure. 'The chocolate box is full and soon it's time to feast again,' he sang to himself.

His eyes widened with imagination. He rubbed his pointed chin and he thought of Elizabeth Dawson.

*

Elizabeth was alone in her penthouse staring mindlessly out over the harbour. Her desk was full of untouched paperwork. A vacant smile swept suddenly across her pretty face. She was so much looking forward to seeing Sebastian again.

# Chapter 10

The moon was just beyond full, waning and rising behind Leslie's laboratory. It was a rarity to see the heavens these past few months but there she was, nonetheless, the faithful old moon, doggedly on patrol as she had been for billions of years, keeping her grim vigil around the Earth, silent and alone.

In spite of this romantic vision, Leslie cursed her for shedding too much light upon him as he and Johannes quietly made their way behind the building and entered through a back entrance that Leslie had discovered by chance some time ago. He figured that the guards would be out the front unaware of his back door. And he was right.

Once inside, he and Johannes crept unhindered down the hallway and into the radio room. Leslie made Johannes sit in the corner while he looked around.

He checked the clock upon the wall. It was almost eleven. He scoured the room to see what he could find but there was nothing of any significance. He scribbled down the precise co-ordinates that guided his satellite dish. He looked at the clock again and he wished the minutes away. He hoped against all hope that Elizabeth and Sebastian didn't frequent the radio room every night at this time to speak with other cities. He needed at least one solid hour of radio contact with the outside world to try to convince someone that democracy was in trouble in Corporate City. What these distant governments could do to help, he had no idea, but he must try. If nothing else he must let them know. He must alert them to the quiet but ominous insurrection that he was certain was being perpetrated by Sebastian Levi from within the top levels of power in Corporate City.

'Why did you bring me here?' Johannes whispered. He looked around nervously. 'You could have done all this by yourself.'

'True,' replied Leslie, turning on the radio, 'but I want you to be a witness and if it comes to a fight, I expect you to back me up.'

'A fight?' Johannes echoed.

'Yes, a fight,' Leslie iterated. He turned and looked at Johannes, large and looming in the corner. 'Or are you just all talk?'

This suggestion appeared to make Johannes angry. He sat straighter in his seat. 'I can fight. Never you mind,' he growled.

'Good,' replied Leslie, turning back to the radio set. 'Okay. We'll be online in just a few minutes.'

He rummaged in a draw where he himself had kept his notes and found a writing pad that he didn't recognise. Nor did he recognise the hand in which it was written, but his guess soon turned to certainty when he read the transcripts written within. These were Levi's notes. The transcripts of multiple conversations with a plethora of world cities all attested to it. The presidents and prime ministers referred to him as Consul Levi or simply as Sebastian. But who had written them? There were no recording devices to be found in the room. Levi must have recorded them on a portable device and transcribed them after each call. 'Very meticulous,' thought Leslie, 'and methodical.' There were tens of conversations: some with London; others to Teheran; to Pyongyang; to Beijing; to Yangon. The list went on. The book was thick and full of notes. It must have taken Sebastian Levi all of his time to keep such copious, copperplate records.

Leslie flicked through the transcripts. It appeared that Levi had given the foreign representatives the idea that he had been democratically elected and that he spoke for the administration of Corporate City. Most of the transcripts were pages long but one page had scrawled across it: *The Western Hemisphere can go to hell!* It was as if a madman had suddenly got the book, graffitied it, and then returned it to its original owner who had resumed his earlier, cordial tone without missing a beat.

Leslie was about to read the last entry, when he heard a faint sound become audible in the distance. He listened with his hand trembling above the pages of the book, straining to discern what the noise was. He had never heard a sound exactly like it before. But it was growing louder.

He placed the book back into the drawer and turned to Johannes who was standing now, alarmed at the increasing ruckus. Leslie raised his hand to his mouth and his index finger up to his lips, concentrating with all his might upon the rising din and combing through his mind to match it with anything he had ever heard before. He couldn't. Whatever it was, it was now very close. Leslie hurried into an adjacent room, stood by the window and pulled back the curtain just sufficiently to see the street outside.

A tremendous and noisy machine was landing there. It was like a giant mosquito, hovering metres above the road. Blades whirred above it with a smaller blade whizzing around at right angles on the tail. It was a ramshackle sort of affair. Its metal wasn't painted and it looked like a prototype, but it was efficient enough. It reached the street and a large, armed guard dashed towards it. He opened the door and out jumped Sebastian Levi, resplendent in suit and tie and following him was Elizabeth Dawson, pretty as a picture in her winter jacket. The cacophony of the machine was slowly abating as Sebastian and Elizabeth made their way towards the building.

'Shit!' exclaimed Leslie.

'What?' asked Johannes in a gust of fear. He was

only a metre away from Leslie but had chosen not to look out of the window for himself.

'It's him.'

'Who?'

'Levi,' Leslie replied curtly as he raced past Johannes.

'Who?'

Leslie switched off the radio set then checked the general area to ensure that he had left no traces of his presence. 'Come.' He waved Johannes into a large walk-in wardrobe that adjoined the radio room.

Johannes followed. They closed the swinging, wooden doors to separate themselves from the main room. Together they stood behind the doors, silently jockeying for best advantage of the view through the wooden slats carved into them.

It wasn't long before they saw Sebastian approach the radio set. They were looking at his back. He switched on the set. Immediately it came to life. Sebastian paused for a moment, perhaps surprised at the speed with which it had warmed up. He seemed to dismiss the thought, however, and turned to address Elizabeth who was now directly behind him.

'Sit,' he ordered and she did, in the seat just occupied by Johannes.

'Sit?' muttered Leslie, amazed at the rudeness of the order and at Elizabeth's readiness to obey it.

Sebastian sat beside the desk, pulled out his transcript book, pulled a pen from his top pocket and opened the book to the next available blank page.

Leslie looked on in wonder as Sebastian Levi began a long conference conversation with Pyongyang, Kabul and Teheran. Leslie couldn't understand what the conversations were about because Levi was somehow able to speak in their native tongues. He appeared to be selling something to each government, because every so often he would mention a price and he repeatedly used the term 'units'. But what most impressed Leslie, as he watched the magnificently confident Levi, all swarthy and dark-eyed in his dark suit and tie, was the efficiency with which he not only presided over the conversation, but the ease with which he also simultaneously wrote out the entire transcript of all parties as the conversation occurred. Page after page he wrote, presumably in the same copperplate hand, whilst quoting technical details to convince whoever he was speaking to that he could achieve whatever it was he had obviously claimed in previous conversations: not only that, but since none of the voices on the other end of the satellite link were speaking in English, Levi must be translating his notes into English in real time and at the same time running the conference. It was startling – and enormously worrying.

After twenty minutes or so, through which Elizabeth had not moved a muscle or contributed one word, Levi ended the conference and replaced the book into the desk drawer. Elizabeth sat, motionless, to one side. She reminded Leslie of an obedient, well-trained dog.

But as Sebastian stood and stretched his back Johannes made a small movement that resulted in a barely audible noise. Levi heard it.

'What was that?' he whispered. Cautiously, he moved towards the slatted swinging doors. Then with a massive thrust, he opened them. He turned on the light. Nothing. He took one step into the wardrobe and crinkled up his nose. 'It stinks in here,' he said. 'Smells like rat shit.' He turned from the doors and towards Elizabeth. 'Come,' he ordered and she followed him from the room.

In the deep recess of the wardrobe Leslie sat with his hand clasped lightly over Johannes' mouth. He removed it. 'You do stink,' he commented.

Leslie listened as the strange machine started up on the road outside. And he continued to listen as its whelping, yawning whistle disappeared into the background night.

He re-entered the radio room and stared down at the drawer for a while. Should he take the book? He wasn't sure. If he took it Levi would know it was probably him. He couldn't risk it. He must return at some other time to read it fully, but he couldn't resist taking one quick look at the English translation of the conversation he had just heard.

He turned to the last entry and his eyes were at once drawn to one isolated section of numbers. It read: Teheran – 20; Pyongyang – 20; Kabul – 10.

The top of the column, under which these numbers were listed, was headed: 'I.Q. Transference Units'.

The manufacturing company was clearly listed further up the same page: Hill Enterprises.

*

'So why the hell didn't you tell me?'

'Steady on.'

'I will not steady on. Why didn't you tell me?'

Leslie was furious with Damien. Johannes listened on with interest.

'Because I don't want to die. Okay? Is that a good enough reason for you?' Damien was walking around his apartment like a caged lion.

'You could have told me. I thought you were my friend. How long have you been working for him?'

Damien stopped walking and stood face to face with Leslie. 'A couple of weeks.'

'What?' Leslie squealed. 'What about our project? Or have you shelved that?'

'No, but mate, this is a royal bloody edict. I can't refuse. They've got me making those transference units twenty-four hours a day.'

'For God's sake!' Leslie blurted, more out of exasperation than anger.

Damien caught him by the elbow. 'Listen, I've been trying to tell you – things are getting very dangerous around here.'

'And what about that thing . . . that helicopter thing? I suppose you made that for that evil bastard from his precious blueprints too, did you?'

'Les,' Damien said quietly, but emphatically, 'I didn't build the damn thing. He did. He welded it together in one of my factories. He built the engine up from nothing. I've never seen anything like it.'

Leslie blinked. He thought back to the radio room. 'He built it?'

Damien nodded. 'In a couple of days. From the ground up.'

Leslie moved towards the scraper window. He looked out over the city lights. He imagined the rich in the scrapers and the poor on the streets. He imagined a better world where there was less inequality. He sifted through his mind and tried to find such a place in history. He found none. In his mind he listened to the Marxist chant of the big red bearded man, who was no doubt watching him right at this moment as he stared out of the window. And he shook his head with sorrow at the realisation that Mao's idea of continuous revolution could never be a possibility in a part of the universe where humans had individual stomachs and minds and where those who rule grow very keen, very quickly, on keeping the status quo. And he thought about Sebastian Levi – what had Damien quipped? - the Rasputin in the queen's ear, was it? And he realised what he had suspected for some time – that Sebastian Levi, librarian, had risen above his station and in a blaze of opportunity, that he, Leslie, idiot consul and inventor, had largely and unwittingly provided, had fed his mind upon the honey dew of others and was about to bring about a social change Karl Marx could only have dreamed of, but for all the wrong reasons and ultimately, with all the wrong results.

He turned back to face Damien and Johannes who had watched his rumination patiently from a distance. 'We have to stop him,' he said.

There was a sudden noise in the corridor outside of the room. Damien and Leslie shared eye contact. Was this the police?

Edgar burst through the door with tears streaming down his fine-featured face. He staggered towards Leslie, reached him, looked desperately into his eyes and uttered in broken gasps, 'Dad's dead.' He buried his face into Leslie's chest and sobbed like a young woman betrayed by her first lover.

Leslie embraced him. He looked towards Damien and then towards Johannes. Both looked downward.

For some time the apartment was wrenched with the sound of human sorrow. Grief, that greatest plague of man, permeated the room as the young man wailed for the loss of his father, the volume of his agony muffled by Leslie's body.

When at last the tears would flow no more, for even tears have a limit, he raised his eyes for comfort and looked up towards Leslie.

'It was arsenic,' said Leslie, in response to Edgar's silent question. This renewed the young man's tears.

When, once again they subsided, Leslie sat him down. He sat beside him. 'Your father was poisoned,' said Leslie, quietly, 'and we're going to find out who was responsible. I promise you. Come on. I'll take you back to my apartment.'

'No you can't,' Edgar replied, suddenly free of grief and full of urgency.

'Why not?'

'Because they're everywhere.'

'What do you mean?'

'At your apartment – there are men everywhere. Police. Big, dumb police. I saw them taking things from your room.'

'What sort of things?' Leslie asked, the indignation growing within him.

'Everything. Furniture. Everything,' Edgar replied, grasping on to Leslie as if not to let him go there.

'What does this mean?' Johannes asked.

Damien answered for Leslie. 'It means, old chum, that the game is up. They're on to you.'

'Levi knew that we were there tonight,' said Leslie. His eyes were quietly alive with realisation. Suddenly he stood. 'Quickly. We must get away before we incriminate you, Damien, and you, Edgar.'

Damien laughed and raised his eyes to the ceiling. 'I think it's a bit late for that now, mate.'

Johannes stepped forward. 'What about my wife and child?'

'They were taken away,' replied Edgar, his eyes soft and sad like a puppy's. 'I don't know where.'

'They're in danger,' replied Leslie, looking towards Johannes with pent fury in his eyes. He thought - 'What can I do?' He moved instinctively once again towards the window and the space that this afforded his caged mind.

'We go to the library,' replied Johannes. 'We go to the library if that's where he's taken them. Is it?'

'Yes,' Leslie replied. 'Almost certainly.'

'Then we go to library and we save them.'

'But how can we get in?' asked Leslie, 'The whole damn place is crawling with police. It has been all week. It'll be covered in them now.'

'We use a back door,' Johannes replied.

'And you know one?' asked Leslie, off-hand, as if he knew the answer already.

'Yes, I do,' the large man replied, unexpectedly. 'And I'm going there right now, with you bastards, or without you.'

# Chapter 11

The electricity buzzed and crackled. Elizabeth's eyes widened and lost some of their lustre. Above, in the console room, Sebastian watched a stream of numbers flow across his computer screen.

'And how do you feel, my dear,' he asked her as she joined him beside the console.

'I don't know,' she replied uncertainly. 'Okay, I think.'

'Excellent. Now it's my turn. It's all set up. All you have to do is push this button.' He pointed to the console.

Elizabeth stared at him vacantly. He laughed lightly and repeated, 'This button, my dear.'

This time she saw the button and nodded.

'This is the big one,' he explained. 'I'm doubling my I.Q. to 1000.'

He may as well have not spoken. Elizabeth looked back at him with bovine serenity.

Sebastian entered the transference room and attached himself to the metal headpiece. He waved his hand. Elizabeth took the cue. She pushed the button.

Below them, crawling through the old Tank Stream, were Leslie, Damien, Johannes and Edgar. Johannes was holding a torch and leading the way. 'This was the city's water supply about four hundred years ago,' he explained. 'About a hundred years ago, after the bombs, a group of people used to live down here.'

'How do you know all this?' asked Leslie, suddenly reefing some cobweb from the side of his mouth.

'Because I'm a well-read man.' He hesitated, 'Also, I've hidden down here from the police a few times.'

Ahead was a breach in the ancient stone. The four men crawled through it, until at last they found themselves ascending into a dark, disused corridor. They moved slowly in the darkness, guided only by the faint light of Johannes' torch. Eventually, they reached a door. It was the door under which Weena had felt the first pangs of love for Rueben well over one hundred years before. Quietly they stepped into the lowest level of the library, surrounded by magazines stacked to a man's height.

Johannes turned off the torch. 'Where to?'

Leslie led the way and onward they trod. He remembered approximately where the room was but he remembered also that it was concealed. So he must be cautious not to miss it.

He need not have worried. Almost immediately he saw a light ahead. Its shaft was emanating from the room he sought. Unfortunately, illuminated by it was a very large man, holding a rifle. He stood with his back to the source of light and stared obediently forward into the gloom of the musty, old library.

'There's a guard,' whispered Leslie, holding the others back with his extended arm. 'He's got a gun.'

'Out of my way,' stated Johannes. And before anyone could stop him, he had marched down the corridor and approached the guard who, as the other three men could clearly see, was now holding his rifle menacingly towards his chest.

Johannes raised his hands as if to surrender and immediately the guard motioned with his rifle for Johannes to enter the room behind him. But at this instant, just as the guard cocked his gun ever so slightly at an angle away from Johannes' body, the Viking-like man grabbed the rifle with both hands, thrust the butt directly into the guard's face, pulverising his nose, and then, before the guard could regain his senses, Johannes slipped behind him, pulled the rifle hard up into the man's throat and strangled him with his own weapon. Silently, the guard slumped to the floor; dead.

Leslie and the others crept up and looked down at the fallen man.

'Can't fight, eh?' Johannes whispered to Leslie.

Leslie placed his hand on his back in silent apology.

Within the lighted room was all crackle and electrical hum. The men moved cautiously into the space. Johannes held the fallen guard's gun at the ready. There was an interior door before them and a stairwell to their left. From beyond the door ahead came a sudden flash of light, accompanied by a loud guttural scream. It was a human sound, but it sounded something between an animal in inestimable pain and a man in the throes of massive orgasm.

Whatever it was, Johannes was in no mood to procrastinate. He turned the door handle, left the door ajar and kicked it with all his might. It swang so hard that it knocked back into his body as he raced into the room, rifle at the ready.

There he found Sebastian leaning back into his chair with a metal helmet attached to his head. His mouth was hanging open and his eyes were glazed with a dream-like aura, as if he had reached a sudden satori and had not quite yet returned. He shook his head, blinked and turned his eyes towards the four intruders as they entered the room. Slowly he removed the metal headpiece.

'One thousand,' he muttered. 'It's all so simple really.'

'What are talking about, Levi?' asked Leslie.

'My name's not Levi, boy,' replied Sebastian.

'Then what is it? Stalin?'

'Oh yes. How clever. An allusion. Man of steel. Yes, I like that. Like superman. It fits.'

'You're talking in riddles, Levi,' Leslie retorted. He had become the group's mouthpiece. Johannes held the gun and stood beside him, but Edgar and Damien kept their distance. There were ominous, raging clouds of anger silently growing beneath the calm exterior of this enigma. They could all feel it. Levi was a gathering storm.

Leslie looked up. He saw Elizabeth standing behind the window to the console room. He looked back to Sebastian for an explanation.

'Oh, I'm sure you've worked it all out, boy,' said Sebastian. 'Clever boy like you. My good friend Elizabeth has very kindly helped me to reach I.Q. 1000. And you wouldn't believe the space in here.'

Leslie looked up again towards Elizabeth. She was suspended in the glass, as still as a portrait. Her eyes were glazed. She was a study in inertia. 'What have you done to her?' he asked, with broken glass in his voice.

'Oh just a few minor modifications,' replied Sebastian with studied nonchalance. 'It's amazing how compliant minds become below about I.Q. 80 – if they're handled carefully.'

'You drained her?'

'Well of course,' replied Sebastian, as if it was the most obvious course of action. 'No man needs a smart wife; an obedient one is preferable. I like to operate on the old Japanese model.'

'You're mad,' Leslie retorted. 'That machine's driven you crazy.'

'Am I?' asked Sebastian, with a slight upturning to one side of his upper lip. 'Am I mad to dumb-down this scheming woman? Am I mad to curb this Lady Macbeth?'

'Elizabeth Dawson is no such thing,' replied Leslie.

'Ah the folly of the human heart,' Sebastian replied, lounging as comfortably as he could upon his metal throne. 'After everything she's done, you still love her. How quaint.'

'She's done nothing wrong except be taken in by

you, you . . . what did you call him, Damien?'

'Rasputin,' added Damien from the rear.

Sebastian laughed loudly at this. He wiped an imaginary tear from his eye for theatrical effect. 'Well, there's certainly some truth in that. I do have a way with the fairer sex - my father always said so. But as for President Dawson, you really have no idea, do you? None of you. No, boy, she's done nothing wrong,' he stood up and looked up towards Elizabeth who was still radiantly beautiful but noticeably inactive in the console room, 'nothing wrong except to steal and hide Colin Dunnett's green book of ideas you so badly sought; nothing wrong except take that book and hide it here in this library for me to find; nothing wrong but play you and your gangly friend here,' he pointed to Damien, 'against one another in the game of love, whilst simultaneously using you both to dream up and engineer designs to consolidate her power; and nothing wrong but poison your father with arsenic, young man,' he pointed at Edgar, 'to make sure that no other consul could share in that power and to make herself, effectively, dictator of Corporate City.'

'You're a liar!' howled Edgar, stepping forward a pace.

'Careful, son,' Sebastian replied, 'I'm not sure of my own strength yet.'

'You *are* lying,' Leslie added. 'Why would Elizabeth steal the book and give it to you?'

'My God. You're so naïve.' Sebastian shook his head and then pointed an accusatory finger up towards Elizabeth in the room above. 'She was no shrinking violet. While you had the chance, rather than ogling over her beauty, you should have asked her about the raids and massacres she's perpetrated upon the few maverick communities in the mountains over the past six years; or about the burning down of old homesteads where any such splinter groups might shelter. The woman was a beautiful monster. She was an expert at removing obstacles. She's had hundreds of people executed over the past few years and she was about to do it again. She was about to begin an anti-Christian campaign to clean them out of the scrapers. That's why she made up those video tapes you saw at the beginning of your term in office.'

'Rubbish,' interjected Leslie, 'we saw Colin Dunnett.'

'Yes, that was real, but the rest was nonsense. She was about to wage a war against the lobby groups who threatened her absolute power. The Christians were her biggest threat. Their numbers have grown and many in the scrapers now profess Christianity. What better way to get at them than to convince her new consuls of the danger they represented to the welfare of the state? Or should I say, the danger they represented to Elizabeth Dawson. She poisoned her other consul to keep him out of the way while she made her plans. Then she played you and this boy off against one another,' he pointed to Damien, 'and had you both scheme up designs to make her look good whilst keeping you out of the way, while she began her attempted manipulation of me. But I outfoxed her. You should be thanking me. I used you to bring her down.'

'Why you?' asked Leslie, who was reluctantly growing to see the merit in Sebastian's argument.

'She buried the book here in the library because she'd read the blueprints and she knew that there was something important hidden somewhere nearby. I guess she figured if anyone would know about it, I would. As it turns out I didn't, until I unscrambled the encrypted message for the map. Then she needed you to get it working, which you did. But you see I no longer need you. I no longer need anyone. Now I'm so brilliant I'm the only person worthy of running this city.'

'Why drain Elizabeth's intelligence?' pursued Leslie.

'She was an immediate threat to my takeover. That and I prefer her as she was.'

'What do you mean?' asked Damien.

'I knew her once upon a time. I knew you too, Damien.'

Damien's cheeks had blanched.

'I see that you're beginning to recall.' Sebastian laughed. 'As I told you, I'm not Sebastian Levi. She, like you, Damien, didn't recognise me after all those years.'

'If you're not Sebastian Levi, then who are you?' asked Leslie.

'My name is Sebastian but it's not Sebastian Levi. You have to take the S and scramble the Levi and you get . . .'

'Viles,' stammered Damien, 'Sebastian Viles.'

'Very good,' replied Viles with a nasty smile.

'That's what I remember. That day over at Elizabeth's apartment - all those years ago - you were there.'

'What a memory you have,' mocked Viles.

'You were there. You were older than us. Something happened that day.'

'Go on, Oedipus. Reveal the awful truth.' Viles' eyes gleamed with mischief.

'You . . . touched her.'

'I always did have a hold on her – emotionally.'

'I remember now.' Damien was stunned at his own revelation. He stared at Viles uncomprehendingly. 'I'd buried the memory away, until now.'

'Yes, and so did she for a time, but when her influential father found out about it a few years later he had me incarcerated for ten years. I was lucky – the old man had more compassion than his daughter. If

Elizabeth had been in charge I'd have been executed for sure. When I finally got out, I took on another persona and I ended up in this foul library dredging through the dregs of history, rather than running this city as my father had done and as I should have continued to do.'

'She was only a little girl,' whispered Damien.

'I was only a boy myself.'

'You were old enough to know better.'

'She was as beautiful then as she is now – more so. She wanted it too. She kissed me back. I used to visit her regularly. She loved me then and she loved me still when I kissed her again over twenty years later.'

'You can't justify that, you prick!' shouted Johannes, levelling the rifle directly at Viles' chest. 'Now, what have you done with my family?'

'They're dead!' Viles screamed with the sudden snarl of the lion and before Johannes could pull the trigger Viles held out his arm with his palm flat, as if he meant Johannes to stop. But as he did, a shock wave of some sort emanated from his hand and Johannes was blasted with a whiplash crack back up against the wall. He dropped the rifle. Viles looked at his hand momentarily, surprised at its new-found power, then he turned it back towards Johannes and raised it upward. Johannes' unconscious body rose up the wall as if roughly picked up by some invisible pair of hands. There he hung suspended for a short while until Viles twisted and clicked his fingers abruptly as if twisting an invisible chicken neck. With an audible 'Crack!' Johannes' head was thrown to one side and his neck snapped clean. His head dropped well below the line of his shoulders. Viles' dropped his hand and down dropped Johannes' body against the wall, a crumpled and dead thing. Viles looked at his hand once again. His eyes were wide with fascination and excitement.

Involuntarily, Leslie, Edgar and Damien stepped

away from the madman and his supernatural display. They were wide-eyed and speechless. Viles thought this amusing.

'For the times they are a changin', boys,' he said with a sneer. He looked at his hand, enamoured with his new-found powers. 'Soon Corporate City will overflow with the riches that will come from sales of my invention.'

'Your invention?' uttered Leslie.

'Well, *I* know it was Dunnett's invention and *you* know it was Dunnett's invention, but history is a matter of opinion, son,' Viles replied, 'and it's my opinion that counts on this occasion. My transference units will change the social structure of every city that embraces them.'

'What are you going to do with us?' asked Damien, quietly eyeing and assessing this empowered lunatic.

'Throw you in gaol until I think of some novel way of disposing of you. But I don't want you all to die just yet. I want you to see the beginnings of my empire before you check out.' He yelled loudly up towards Elizabeth, 'Get down here!' And her face immediately disappeared from the window above. 'You see, I have such plans. And I'd like you to see how they're progressing in a few years' time before I'm rid of you.'

Elizabeth entered the room with a vacuous smile. She was as beautiful as ever, but her usually sparkling eyes were somehow duller; less cast out into the world. She took up her place beside Viles.

'Ah, here she is,' Viles said loudly, kissing her upon the forehead. 'Can you see it?' he asked.

'See what?' asked Leslie.

'Why, the baby bump of course. My darling Elizabeth is with child, aren't you, my dear?'

Elizabeth smiled and nestled in, under Viles' arm.

'Yes, he continued, 'we're going to have a little

baby-Viles and the Viles are going to rule this city for a long time to come - and possibly even other cities too, given time.'

Several large men arrived at the door. 'Ah, it's about time,' said Viles. Take these men away.'

'We'll beat you,' whispered Leslie, as the guards pinned back his arms.

'One day,' added Edgar, 'one day we'll win.'

'No you won't,' replied Viles.

And Leslie, Damien and Edgar were roughly bundled from the room.

# Chapter 12

MONTAGE

Leslie sits upon straw in a dark cell. One small embrasure lets in a single shaft of light upon his face.

Viles works at his desk in his apartment. Behind him the harbour can be seen. In the foreground his son, now a toddler, is trying to walk towards Elizabeth. She smiles with maternal joy.

In quick succession, JUMP CUTS of metal caps and I.Q. transfers. Some walk out rejuvenated; others blank behind the eyes.

In the streets of Corporate City electric motor scooters are in abundance.

Many small yellow electric cars can also be seen.

In the gambling casinos people in rags sit at a seemingly endless line of I.Q. gambling machines.

Viles hands some blueprints to an engineer who nods and exits. We see a maze under construction. Metal thrusts up from below ground level in a variety of dancing slats.

A seething throng of people sit in a large arena around one of those mazes. There is great excitement as one man in rags dodges into the maze and appears at another point to shoot another. Viles claps his hand and laughs. Beside him Elizabeth and their boy, now about seven, laugh and applaud.

At the mouth of the harbour a giant structure is being constructed. It spans from head-to-head. On either side of it and stretching out north and south is a giant metal wall, also under construction.

Edgar sees Damien and Leslie in the exercise yard. All three are emaciated and weak. Leslie nods down towards the harbour. Edgar follows the line of his nod. He watches as a large container ship enters the harbour.

*

Leslie, Edgar and Damien were thrown into a room by a bunch of hairy-knuckled guards. They each collected themselves from the floor and found their way towards the window. They looked down.

Edgar nodded towards the harbour's heads. A huge metal structure spanned from north to south across the mouth separating the harbour itself from the great ocean beyond. It was a massive coil of rolled up steel; a huge cylinder hanging heavily above the two outcrops of land. Extending from it in both directions was a great wall, stories high. Hundreds upon hundreds of workers were dotted in and around it. It seemed to be growing as the men watched on.

Inside the harbour, a large container ship loaded cargo. The great ship bore the Union Jack and proclaimed the vessel: 'The British Lion'. In the foreground, and directly beneath the trio, was a large area of dirt, curiously scarred by straight lines - some running parallel, others at right angles to these. Looking down on this dirt arena from the side where the men were, was a gentle grass hill with seating carved into it. On the other three sides were makeshift trestles and seats, tiered around.

The three men were too weak to embrace one another. They were ragged and wretched but they still managed to raise their arms around each other's shoulders. As one defiant unit they stared, their eyes blinking under the brightness of the summer day. Silently, they gazed out across the vista.

Viles entered. He was visibly older and he had grown more portly in his middle age. His face was more jowly and his stomach more rotund. But the same dark eyes were there, locked behind his glasses.

'Sit,' he ordered. And the three men did so, without a qualm.

'Aha,' said Viles as he sat beside the window, 'obedience born of deprivation and routine. You're all institutionalised.'

None of the men contested this. None of them was in a position to contest anything.

'You've no doubt noticed the wall?' Viles enquired, as he scribbled something down upon a pad of paper. 'It will soon encompass the entire city. When it's completed no one will get in, or out, without my consent. You'll also be interested to know that the few mavericks in the mountains are no more. Napalm is such a simple but effective cleanser.'

Viles grinned without malice. His eyes poked over the rims of his glasses. 'Perhaps you'd like to see yourselves?' he said, nodding to a large wall mirror behind the men that they had not yet noticed.

The three of them turned. Edgar's neck shot back with surprise and he began to cry.

'Yes, it's a bit of a shock, I expect. Haven't seen yourself for eight years. The three of you are a little scrawny and a deal older too.'

Leslie marvelled at the vision. All three of them were bones with meat attached. All three were bearded and grimy. All three were so much older. He knew that they all stank, just as Johannes had stank all those years ago, but he was well beyond smelling it.

'You're lucky,' smirked their tormentor, 'while you've been relaxing in incarceration, I've been working endlessly to structure the new world. And not just in Corporate City, God no – all over the planet. I've been co-ordinating imports and exports and . . .' He stopped. He saw the utter disinterest inscribed upon the faces before him. 'But I see that I'm boring you. So, I'll get to the point.'

He stood and stared out across the great wide harbour. Behind him, the three captives watched his silhouette with silent attention.

'I'm offering one of you a chance at life.'

The men looked from one to the other.

'Just one,' Viles continued. 'I have some games scheduled here for tomorrow night. If you're lucky, very lucky, one of you may walk out of this place tomorrow night a free man.' He paused for effect. 'You see, this city has been transformed in your absence. It seems that if you give some men a hundred dollars, they'll be rich within a year, while others will be poverty stricken within a week. Such are the vagaries of free choice. And so it is that there are those in this city who have traded their I.Q. unwisely, while others have profited from the foolishness of their fellow man.' He turned and moved closer to his audience. 'I cannot, of course, allow a great flourishing of mind because it would impair my ability to govern, so I've limited I.Q. to 300 points; but neither can I afford to preside over a city full of idiots, so conversely I must dispose of those who sink to idiocy because of, well, their idiocy.'

As Leslie listened, the hatred grew within him.

'So I've come up with this idea. I call it the I.Q. Games. I won't go into the details. However, I have a special guest visiting tomorrow night and I wish to impress him. You all have a choice. You can remain in your cells for the rest of your natural days, or you can take part in this great sporting event tomorrow evening.'

'Go on,' said Damien. He spoke for all of them. Better to die in some sporting contest than to languish, barely alive, in the semi-darkness in a rabbit's cage for the rest of one's years.

'Very well,' Viles replied. 'Stand.'

And they did.

'Look here.'

They moved back towards the window.

'The spot we occupy now was once a great zoo. Can you believe it? A great zoo. Where animals were given the best view in this city. Animals! Creatures even more pathetic than you!'

If Viles wanted a response from these three weakened animals he had to do better than that.

'Look down upon this arena,' stated Viles with a nod towards the area the men had been looking at before. 'And look very closely.'

Viles pushed a button. Vertical slats of metal simultaneously thrust upward; some were parallel, some were at right angles to the three men's point of view.

Viles explained, 'This maze has a multitude of configurations. This is the one we will be using tomorrow night. I want you to look at it very carefully, gentlemen, because this is the only time that you will see it before The Games begin.'

Edgar, and Damien looked hard at the configuration of metal. Leslie also looked out, but he looked beyond the maze to the grounds leading down to the harbour on the far side.

'Tomorrow, just before the contest, I will show this same configuration to another five men. Each of these men is an I.Q. 300. Each of these men wants to gain power under my wing. I have promised the man who walks from that maze power second only to my own. But only one man will walk from that maze tomorrow night.'

He turned and looked closely at the three. 'Remember what you can of the labyrinth, men, because I can assure you that each of the men I show this to tomorrow will instantly remember its every turn.'

A young boy of seven or eight burst his way into the room and dived upon Viles' leg. Viles appeared embarrassed. He removed the boy as one might extricate a leech.

'Ah Christopher,' he said, 'what are you doing here?'

'Mummy's here,' answered the boy and sure enough the door opened and in walked Elizabeth. She was elegant in a white summer frock and matching wide-brimmed hat. She was a little older, perhaps, but still beautiful.

She looked at the three men without recognition.

'You remember Damien and Leslie?' asked Viles.

'Vaguely,' she replied.

Leslie felt tears well up into the corners of his eyes. He watched Elizabeth move as if she was in a slow-motion dream. Gone was the powerful presence; gone was the charismatic leader. His tears made their way down the deep creases beneath his eyes and dropped upon the unforgiving floor.

'I'm hardly surprised,' Viles continued, 'it was some time ago. And they have lost a little weight. Now take Christopher and wait for me downstairs. We have people to meet.'

'Yes, Sebastian,' she replied obediently. She nodded to Leslie as she left. 'Come, Christopher.'

'Are these men all going to die tomorrow night?' asked Christopher, as his mother took his hand.

'Probably,' replied Viles.

'Oh good,' he trumpeted.

And they left.

'That's my boy,' said Viles.

# Chapter 13

The summer evening fell and the tired sun cast its surreal light across the harbour at the tail end of a hot Australian summer day. A southerly had mercifully blown in and it swept its cool relief through the heads and up the hill towards the crowd gathering in the arena. A large banner was plastered at the back of one stand proclaiming the occasion: 'The Taronga Park Games'. Men wore hats, shorts and collared shirts; women wore bright summer hats and light cotton dresses which were blown alluringly by the blustery wind. The sun was coming to rest behind the hills, well beyond the great Coathanger Bridge. The lights were taking over, and the crowd was settling.

The expensive seats were carved into the hill on the northern side of the arena. These looked down upon the harbour and the greater part of the city on its southern side. For the first time though, money was not enough to buy an individual a seat in this area. It was expensive, yes, but the determining factor was I.Q. A sign at the entrance to the stand clearly stated 1.Q. 200+ and a group of heavily armed guards were at the entrance checking the relevant documentation. One 150 did try to sneak in but he was caught. He was later drained 10 I.Q. points as a fine.

Viles entered, followed quietly by Elizabeth and Christopher who took up their seats to one side. There was great applause as Viles waved to the crowd. He had already learned the lessons of the dictator: keep the masses happy with meaningless diversion; control the press; keep your army happy; and destroy all potential enemies before they even realise that you think they are a threat. So, the masses waved and yelped; the press was limited to reporting the bare facts, embellished with some hyperbole for President Viles; the army was out in force, well-fed, rich in money, but poor in 1.Q. (by government regulation) and any opposition that had come to the attention of the president, vaporised and stored as I.Q. in black boxes in console rooms throughout the city.

As the cheers went up for the president, he heralded in his guest for the evening and the crowd responded as they knew their president wished, by cheering for him also. His name was Kim Benny Jong Il – one of a long line of Kims. He was a small but rotund man of Asian appearance. His cheekbones were high, as those from farther north. His face smiled but his eyes were dead; he waved his hand but the gesture was empty. He was here to do business with Viles and this sideshow was a necessary business obligation. He sat next to Viles.

'How do you like my city?' asked Viles in Korean.

'Too many flies,' Jong Il replied in his native tongue.

Viles tried again, 'I trust you will enjoy tonight's games.'

'A waste of I.Q,' was the reply.

'If you purchase the quota of transference machines you have pledged to buy then you will never have to waste any I.Q. again,' said Viles. 'Instead of wasting all that I.Q. in your gas chambers you will be able to store it. You will be able to kill your people but their I.Q. will still bring you profit.'

'We shall see,' was the reply.

Benny Jong Il sat stiffly like a regent condescending to be present. Viles loathed the pompous little prick, but business is business.

'I have looked around the streets of your city. You have many poor,' he said.

'Yes,' replied Viles. 'What of it?'

'Too many poor mean too many trouble,' replied Jong Il. 'Better you support the middle. Give them necessities. Keep content through ignorance. Like religion. Control through I.Q.'

Viles stiffened with thought. 'I understand,' he replied. And a light turned on in his mind. Then he added, 'Your forefathers were renowned for malnourishing their people whilst keeping their total allegiance. I believe that even by the early years of the twenty first century the people of the north were several centimetres shorter than the people from the south, even though they were originally from exactly the same genetic stock?'

'You are well read,' replied Jong Il. 'I am proud to say that my people grow smaller every decade.'

Viles laughed but secretly wished the little turd would disappear up his own arsehole. And so the unpleasantries continued until, at eight o'clock, The Games began.

At this stage, the arena was nothing but an open dirt floor, perhaps one hundred metres by fifty and levelled for the contest. The maze was below ground, waiting for its chance to jump to life.

Five fine young men stepped into the arena, rapturously applauded by the crowd. They were all in their prime, between twenty and thirty, all of strong build and all had purchased brilliant minds. Each wore a different coloured lightweight jersey, the colours of the spectrum from red to blue, so they could be easily distinguished by the spectators. As one, they saluted the president and his guest. Then each held up the gun they were about to use in the upcoming contest. Again, the crowd roared.

Leslie, Damien and Edgar looked down upon the arena from the room in which they had spoken to Viles the day before. They had just been reunited and they were still dressed in the grey uniform of Corporate City criminals.

'It looks like this is it,' said Damien, turning to the others.

'I hope you remember the maze configuration,' said Edgar, 'because I sure as hell don't.'

'I wouldn't have a clue,' Damien replied. 'What about you, Les? You're the only one of us smart enough to remember the maze.'

Leslie, who had moved apart from the other two and who was staring at something below, replied absent-mindedly, 'Oh, no, I wouldn't have a clue. I wasn't even looking at it.'

'You weren't looking at it?' repeated Damien. He moved towards Leslie. Edgar followed him. 'Mate, your life depends on it.'

Leslie turned on them urgently. 'Listen to me. It doesn't matter about the maze. There's no way any of us are going to survive.'

'But . . .' began Damien.

'No. You must listen,' interrupted Leslie. 'In the unlikely event that any of us is alive at the end of this thing, Viles will kill us anyway. Now, look here.' He pointed to the far side of the arena. 'Take note. The far stand is a temporary one, built for this occasion. If you look closely, you'll see that there is a small breach in the fence about halfway along. See?'

Damien and Edgar squinted and eventually saw the spot. They nodded.

'Good. Now, listen. We don't have much time. I know this place. Behind that stand there's a hill sloping down to the harbour and if my memory serves me correctly there's a wharf at the bottom. If we're lucky, there might be a boat moored there.'

'How do we get there?' asked Edgar.

'We work as a team. We don't stray too far from one another and we make a bolt through that cavity whenever we get the chance. If there are guards, we surprise them and knock 'em out of the way. Simple as that.'

'What about the maze?'

'If it's in the way we'll have to make our way around the outside.'

The others looked uncertain.

'Look. This is our only chance.'

'And if there's no boat?' Damien asked.

'There's a vast bushland further south, down towards Bradley's Head. There's another wharf there. Listen. They won't be expecting this. Viles is expecting us to be trying to blow each other's head off and they won't have any guards down there behind that temporary stand. Why would they? We've got the element of surprise on our side.'

He looked hopefully towards the two men. Though far from convinced, they both agreed that it was their only hope.

'Good,' said Leslie. 'Just remember to stay alive long enough to make a run for it. These other men will be very smart.'

'But you're smart too,' said Edgar.

'Thanks, mate,' Leslie replied with a smile, 'but I only come in somewhere in the 150s.'

'So each of those men is twice as smart as you?' asked Edgar, despondently.

'Unfortunately not,' Leslie replied. 'I.Q. is exponential. Each point increases your intelligence by a lot. They're hundreds of times smarter than me.'

'Great,' said Damien.

The door burst open and a dozen guards herded the trio back through it, down a long series of corridors and out into the floodlighted brightness of the arena. It was twilight now, as the three men joined the other five in front of the president. Each was given a gun.

Viles' mind was alight with the movement and

countermovement of hypothetical men in the hypothetical maze he was viewing in his mind. He played at possibilities in his visual cortex at such speed that the five colours of the contestants melded into a rainbow of possibilities, like ten-thousand-time lapse vehicles in New York, viewed from above. The three grey prisoners were so insignificant that he did not even bother to factor them in to his computations.

Behind the eight combatants, with an enormous 'whoosh', the metal slats sprang skyward and the maze was up. The crowd exploded. All eight men were taken to separate places around the arena on the outside of the maze to await the starting siren.

There was great anticipation in the crowd and a silence fell upon it. But the tension was released into laughter when 'The British Lion', departing for northern waters, sounded her horn in the harbour and some in the audience thought that the bout had begun. After this prematurity and much laughter from the crowd, the siren did eventually sound and The Games began in earnest.

Immediately the five 300s entered their nearest entrance to the maze. Each, with the mind of a genius, realised that they must first kill off the serious competition before they bothered mopping up the criminals Viles had thrown in as, as they saw it, a kind of carnival curiosity. No, first they must survive the onslaught of the other 300s. Then they could worry about the other three also-rans. Inside each of their minds was a blueprint of the labyrinth and, as each saw an overview of the map in their mind, each played out the various routes that the others might take and assessed the ramifications of those moves. Like five master chess players, the five-armed men moved noiselessly within the metal walls, each watching the configuration of the maze from a bird's eye point of view within the fluid compartments of their lock-step minds.

Meanwhile, Leslie, Damien and Edgar, who had watched the 300s enter the maze, chose not to enter it. They ran around its outside and met up on the far side of it to Viles. They stood as a group, each with his gun pointed outward. Slowly, under Leslie's guidance, they were shuffling towards the area of the fence where he had seen the breach. This small knot of men shuffling along the outside of the maze and its contrast to the stealthy movement and counter movement of the five men within it began to cause a rumble in the crowd.

Some members of the audience saw the farce in it and pointed this out to others. Many crowd members began to titter and even to laugh openly at the contradiction between the behaviour of the geniuses in the maze and that of the lower I.Q.s on the outside. This sheer juxtaposition was funny enough, but when the red and blue 300s managed to find themselves face to face within the maze and managed to blow each other's heads off, the contrast became clear to all, and hoots of laughter permeated the arena.

'It seems that your idiots are smarter than your geniuses,' the interpreter translated for Benny Jong Il.

Viles nodded and smiled at Jong Il but he was highly embarrassed, a fact that the Korean dictator well realised – and he was dining heartily on schadenfreude.

'What's happening?' asked Christopher of his mother, but Elizabeth was hardly there. Gone were the flashing eyes, gone was the passionate potentate. She was a shell; an ornament; an empty thing; a child.

Leslie, Damien and Edgar reached the small breach in the fence. Damien had a quick look, so as not to make their intentions too obvious.

'There's a small gap we can fit through one at a time and there's a passageway behind it leading through the grandstand, but there's a problem.'

'What's that?' asked Leslie who had not taken his eyes from the maze in front of him for fear of the sudden appearance of a 300.

'There are about seven or eight guards on either side of it.'

'It figures,' said Edgar. He was breathing heavily and sweating profusely. Damien steadied him by the arm.

'It's okay, boy. We'll get you through. Les, how many bullets do we have?'

'These are six shooters, I think.'

'We have eighteen bullets,' said Damien.

The three men looked one to the other.

'Better make 'em count.'

Behind them, in the maze, a barrage of shots rang out and a high-pitched scream told that another 300 had been hit. This galvanised them into action.

The three men placed their hands together for luck. Their eyes met and they each tried to smile. They broke hands, left their little silent world, and turned towards the crowd. The noise was deafening. Some were cheering the winning combatants in the maze; others had grown tired of the trio's lack of participation and were beginning to jeer loudly; and yet others still found the whole thing hilarious and were belly-laughing like hyenas.

Into the melee the three men plunged; Damien first, then Leslie, then Edgar, each with their guns ablaze and levelled directly at the guards. Five guards, who had been on crowd control and so had been facing the wrong direction, were killed outright by the hail of bullets. Another two saw their comrades fall, turned and tried to return fire. But they had been caught by surprise and both were felled. Two bystanders were also hit and Edgar felt some compassion for them as he sped past, but his compassion was swamped by his adrenaline and his great desire to live.

Through the dark passageway they sped to be spat out onto the grass hill beyond. Downhill they ran, their hearts pounding in their necks, down towards the harbour.

It took a moment for Viles to realise what had happened. At first, he, like everyone else on the far side of the arena, thought that the barrage of bullets was coming from inside the maze. When he realised the truth, he was livid. He stood and commanded all guards to: 'Kill them! No quarter!' And two score of men left their posts and disappeared into the night.

The moon was not yet up and the going was tough for the three fugitives. Their knees were grazed and their bodies bruised by the time they approached the water.

'There it is!' Leslie whispered loudly. 'Quick!'

Down towards the wharf they ran at breakneck speed and onto the old wooden boards that creaked and boomed with their arrival.

But there was no boat.

'Shit!' Damien cursed.

'There's one out there,' said Edgar, pointing out across the dark water.

The sound of men became audible. The guards were hurrying down the hill just as the fugitives had and, just like the fugitives, they had no lanterns. So there were yells and yelps as some took chunks out of themselves on the rough sandstone, under the moonless night.

'Down here!' said Leslie. He jumped off the wharf and into the harbour. Damien and Leslie followed.

The water was cold, in spite of summer, and the salt ate into their abrasions. Leslie was no great swimmer and the water invaded his nose as he hit the water and he tasted the sea, via his nostrils.

The three men huddled under the wharf, clutching the pylons. The grim sea water lapped against them.

Soon they heard the rumble of boots on suspended boards. They held their breath and listened as one of the guards said, 'Take your men down the southern trail. I'll take mine and head north.' Then they heard the scuttle of boots on boards again, then the sound of disappearing voices and then silence.

'Look,' whispered Edgar. 'That boat. It's coming closer.'

'It's a ferry, thank God,' Damien replied.

'Should we swim for it?' asked Edgar.

'No need,' replied Leslie. 'It'll be here within a couple of minutes. We'll wait for it and commandeer it when it gets here.'

The men resurfaced and clamoured into the night-time silence of the shed above. They dried themselves as best they could. Edgar kept look out, but there was no movement north or south and no one was coming down the hill.

The ferry was about to dock and the captain was throwing out the painters when they heard a cough come from the darkness behind them. They turned to see a solitary guard with his rifle trained upon them. They raised their hands.

'Step over here, into the light,' he commanded. He was a large man with big features and a gruff voice. The men obeyed without protest.

'Let us go,' said Edgar. 'No one will ever know. Please.'

The guard laughed sardonically. 'Now why would I do that?' he asked. 'I'll get two I.Q. points apiece for you runaways and an extra five if I bring you in alive. I'm not allowed to use 'em, but I sure as hell can sell 'em.'

The captain of the ferry had tied her off by this time. He was lonely and pleased for any company. He could just make out the four men in the darkness of the shed. 'Probably get a few strays coming down the hill from the show tonight!' he yelled out in welcome. 'Don't know why they'd bother, to be honest. It's a dark old road. Still I s'ppose some youngens'll try.' He laughed to himself with the thought. He moved towards them. 'Any sane person'd go by electric bus.'

'Go away, old man,' commanded the guard.

'There's no need to be rude, young fella,' replied the old salt, still approaching.

'I said go away!' blurted the guard. As he shouted this, he kicked the poor man viciously in the leg. The old man yelped in pain and fell backwards clutching his shin. But the effort had thrown the guard momentarily off balance. In an instant, Damien grabbed for his gun. He was soon joined in the scuffle by Leslie and Edgar. In amongst the thrashing and the bashing, somehow the gun went off. The thrashing stopped. Damien fell off the pack.

The guard rose to his feet, holding the gun towards Leslie and Edgar, 'Now get up,' he ordered, 'or I'll kill you both!'

Edgar got up, but Leslie knelt above Damien. He turned him over. His grey robes were sodden with red and the stain was growing like a dry riverbed after the first rains.

'Damien,' Leslie cried.

'I said get up!' shouted the guard.

But Damien was gone. His eyes were glazed and dead and the blood was pouring out of him.

'I won't tell you again!' warned the guard.

The guard could not see Leslie's face but a look of pure fury had wiped all other emotion from it and a maelstrom of hatred whirled within each of his eyes. Without a word he found the gun tucked into his trouser sash, ripped it from its hiding place, turned and fell and fired one single shot right into the middle of the guard's forehead. The guard stood for a second, as if unable to believe it, then he crashed, first onto his knees and then onto his face and then, in slow motion, onto the splintery boards.

'We've got to go,' Leslie said urgently. 'Everybody within ten kilometres heard that shot. Quick grab his gun.'

'But Damien?' asked Edgar.

'He's dead, Edgar. Damien's dead.'

Edgar looked down in disbelief.

'And you're going to take us out. Now!' Leslie ordered the ferryman.

'Alright. Alright. I'll take you. I'll take you. Hold your horses,' muttered the ferryman. He looked down at Damien, 'Sorry about your friend,' he said, then as he passed the fallen guard he spat, 'You can go to hell,' he muttered, rubbing his shin and making his way awkwardly towards his vessel.

As they cast off, Leslie and Edgar heard the approach of men coming from south and north.

The engines started up and the ferry pulled away. It was disappearing into the gloom by the time the guards reached the wharf. They fired several shots but it soon became obvious that the ferry was too far out to stop.

'Never mind,' said one captain of the guards, 'we'll be waiting for them on the other side.'

Viles, who had finally divested himself of that self-righteous, gloating Benny Jong Il, who apparently, according to him, never had escapees in his country, was in no great mood by the time this information was relayed to him.

'What!' he screamed at the captain of the guard.

'It's alright, President Viles,' the man assured him, 'we've already got people waiting for them on the other side of the harbour. They can't possibly get away. There's nowhere else to go.'

Viles thought about that for a moment. He turned

and looked out across the harbour. The watery world was in darkness, but for 'The British Lion' who had finally made her way out towards the heads. Her lights dominated the scene.

A phone call came. Viles took it. 'Yes.' He paused and listened. 'What do you mean they're not on board?' He listened again. 'Well check again. Check the hold. Check the . . .' Viles stopped. He turned savagely around and stared back out of the window and across the harbour towards the great British container ship carving her way towards the open sea.

'Damn you to hell!' he blurted. He disconnected the phone and dialled another number. 'South Head!' he barked. 'Bring down the Keeper of the Breach! Now!'

Viles threw the phone at the wall and stood glaring out of his window.

Above the heads, the suspended, rolled metal began to unravel like a creaky old giant waking after a long sleep. Downward she unfurled, screeching all the long way – a roller door of massive proportions.

Beneath her 'The British Lion' was already passing into open sea. Looking up from the aft and resting against a huge container were Leslie and Edgar. They watched as the great metal barrier unfurled to completely encase the harbour and cut it off from the outside world. By that time, the lights of Corporate City were mere froth upon the distant horizon.

'Do you think they'll welcome us in London?' asked Edgar.

'I hope so, Edgar. I hope so. But at least for the minute we're free from the curse of Viles.'

'We'll beat him one day,' said Edgar.

'Maybe,' replied Leslie, 'but maybe not in our lifetime. Come on. Let's get something to eat.'

Leslie placed his arm in friendship around Edgar's shoulder and the two men left the stern together.

*

ANGLE ON to the container upon which they have been leaning.

It reads: I.Q. Transference Unit – Westminster - London.

**This is the end of The DNA Trilogy and the beginning of The I.Q. Trilogy, the first few pages of which follow.**

# PROLOGUE

INT.LOUNGE ROOM.NIGHT

An OLD MAN in a rocking chair sits in front of a fire. He looks down severely upon a YOUNG BOY of nine or ten.

In front of the boy is a small cage within which are two tiny mice. The top of the cage is open and a hammer sits beside it.

                    OLD MAN
          Decide.

The young boy looks from the cage and up to the old man. He is confused.

                    OLD MAN (CONT.)
                 (more emphatically)
          Decide.

ANGLE ON to the hammer and then onto the mice.

The boy is caught in a dilemma. He puts his hand into the cage, picks up the mice and lets them go. He looks up to the old man for a response.

Unexpectedly, the old man lunges forward with his cane and smites the young boy across the cheek.

The boy is knocked sideways. As he sits back up, he holds his hand to his damaged cheek. Blood appears through his hand. He begins to cry.

                    OLD MAN
                 (angrily)
          Don't cry!

The boy stops.

> OLD MAN (CONT.)
> You will learn, Paul, as I have learned and as your father learned before you, that mercy is a weakness of mind which affects only those who are uncertain of total victory. And believe me, boy, it will always come back to bite you.

The old man sits back in his seat. The young boy sits at his feet, desperately trying not to cry.


EXT.CITY STREET.DAY

A MIDDLE-AGED MAN steps out of a limousine onto a grimy street. He leans back into the car and speaks to the same young boy. The boy bears fresh stitches in his cheek.

> MIDDLE-AGED MAN
> Wait.

He moves off.

Filled with curiosity, the young boy gets out of the limo and stands on the pavement, next to the car, taking in the ambience.

It is a poor area. Vagrants abound and homeless people seem to be the norm.

A TEENAGE BOY in ragged clothes steps up to the limo. The young boy turns to face him.

> TEENAGER
> Nice scar, rich boy.

He opens a flick knife.

TEENAGER (CONT.)
Want another one?

Before the teenager can act, two large BODYGUARDS suddenly appear. They wrestle the teenager away from his knife and squash his face hard against the window of the limo.

The middle-aged man returns.

MIDDLE-AGED MAN
Bring him.

Kicking wildly, the teenager is dragged into the building.

PAN UP to the top of the building. We see the letters I.Q.T.C.


INT.I.Q.T.C. DAY

The teenager is strapped into a chair and a metal cap fixed upon his head.

The young boy sits beside him. He also has a metal cap upon his head.

Above them, behind a glass panel, is the middle-aged man. He speaks to the young boy via an intercom loudspeaker.

MIDDLE-AGED MAN
Remember, son, mercy is the only luxury that those in power can't afford.

He smiles. ANGLE ON to his hand. He twists a dial on a console.

MIDDLE-AGED MAN (CONT.)
And to the victor, go the spoils.

There is a loud electrical buzzing sound. The eyes of the teenager widen in extreme close up.


INT.LOUNGE ROOM.NIGHT

The young boy's face has nearly healed. He sits at his desk, pondering over his school books.

In the background ANGLE ON to the empty cage with the hammer sitting upon it.

A sudden noise catches the boy's attention.

Alarmed, he rises and picks up the hammer. He moves cautiously towards the wall. He listens.

Carefully, he pulls back a panel and there is a nest of baby mice.

The boy looks for a moment, startled, and then he laughs, slightly hysterically. His laughter gradually subsides. His face hardens into hatred.

With sudden inspiration, he smashes the hammer down upon the nest with great violence, over and over again.

# Chapter 1

The arena was alive. Twenty thousand people in an enormous, transparent dome. High above their heads, a helicopter descended. Bodyguards jumped onto the flattened central portion of the dome.

President Viles, a thin, middle-aged man, stepped confidently onto the glass surface. His spindly frame was punctuated by the clean fit of his suit. Fine white hands protruded delicately from his cuffs; his face was scrawny, cruel, and lined. His mean etched features supported small, rimless glasses perched upon his bony nose. A deep scar was chiselled into one of his cheeks.

His arm was adorned by a stunning blonde. She was somewhere in her late twenties. She wore an elegant gold dress which clung to her petite, well-proportioned frame. She smiled and flicked back her curls, which blew in the helicopter wind.

Fifty metres below was the playing area - the centre of a doughnut around whose periphery were two tiers of seating - the doughnut itself. A seething throng of spectators swarmed within those tiers. The arena was full.

President Viles extricated the pretty adornment from his arm and whispered something to a bodyguard, who instantly stood aside and erect, like any good soldier  obeying orders. Viles motioned to his beautiful young companion to precede him into their viewing box.

The 'box' was in fact a semi-circle which hung suspended above the central portion of the playing area. It was a tiny bubble blown inside the skin of the major dome. The best seat in the house.

Well below, in the higher of the two tiers, the Carter family was settling in.

Joseph was in his late thirties. He had brown hair, fair skin, was thin and was not very handsome. His nose was a little too pronounced and his jaw rather too angular. He had a little too much of the cartoon character about him: his ears jutted out a little too much and his eyes were a fraction too large for the size of his face.

By contrast, his wife, Josephine, was extremely lovely. She was petite, had short blonde hair, flawless green eyes and her features were as fine as porcelain. She was younger than Joseph by a number of years, a sore point with Joseph and one which Josephine would often exploit with glee. But she loved him with great devotion and though he often wondered what she saw in him, he was ever grateful for her love.

Right now, she was rummaging inside a metal box. Eventually, she produced a sandwich for her husband. He smiled and accepted the gift whilst his children, Marcus, and Miriam, looked at the pictures advertising tonight's show.

At fifteen, Miriam was the older of the two. She was quite pretty and feminine like her mother, although, presumably through the zipper of genetics, she had inherited her father's brown hair and, unfortunately, his pronounced nose also.

Marcus was a robust thirteen-year-old, more nuggetty than his sister and the truth to tell, looked absolutely nothing like the rest of his family. He possessed reddish hair, a freckly complexion, and a rugged smile. Joseph called him his little risk-taker, for Marcus had a semi-reckless disposition, and though his parents made light of this, it was in fact of some concern to them.

But now was time for fun.

The top tier, where they were seated, unlike the lower one, had glass between it and the arena. Joseph had managed to get his family front row seats, so Miriam and Marcus breathed on the glass and drew patterns on their exhalation.

An announcement informed the crowd that President Viles had arrived and that it was time to sing the Corporate Jingle. In one accord the dress circle stood.

In the lower tier they seemed more interested in their beef treats and sugar.

Viles looked down imperiously from his bubble while the insipid, lacklustre tune slid indifferently from the mouths of the lower tier, and in mindless rote from the top. Thirty seconds put an end to it. The president sat. The top tier had to go through the whole process of settling again.

An announcer's voice boomed into the air: 'Welcome to tonight's Glidiot Games. Tonight's crowd - 20,214'. Cheers of satisfaction erupted. In the lower tier the standing masses yelped and wailed. In the dress circle above them the seated masses applauded.

'Everyone loves The Games!' yelled Joseph into his wife's ear.

Josephine nodded and continued to rummage inside a metal box for some lost treat for the children.

A second announcement burst into the air above the cavernous doughnut hole. 'Total I.Q. - 1.75 million.' This was met with less enthusiasm from the lower tier. Jeers and boos reverberated through the enclosure.

'Less than average,' mused Joseph, more to himself than to anyone else. He nibbled at his sandwich.

Marcus had fixed his eyes upon the president, a lifetime away in the bubble above. He nodded towards the president's bubble. 'That doesn't include him though, does it, Dad?'

'No,' he replied. 'They never count the highfliers. As soon as President Viles arrived the arena's Intelligence Quotient went up by 1000.'

'Here they come!' yelped a delighted Miriam.

From her high vantage point behind the glass, she could see a group of Glidiots being led through the crowd beneath and out into the bright austerity of the central portion of the great dome.

They were a motley lot: a ragtag band of misfits, variously dressed, but generally unkempt. The only thing to mark them as a unified group were the flashing, luminous dog collars encircling each of their necks.

'I like the look of that one,' said Marcus, pointing towards a muscular man of six foot something and seemingly half as broad as an acreage. The stubble upon his face had not yet decided to become a beard, but a few more hours would take that decision out of its hands - if he had a few hours.

'He's not bad looking,' mused Josephine. 'I hope he wins.'

Joseph smiled at her with the mock annoyance of one truly secure in a relationship. She laughed and held his hand.

There were twenty-one Glidiots in all. Two thirds were male. Some were tiny, emaciated things, others, obese and shabby. The flashing lights upon their dog collars blinked, and so did they, beneath the severe neon brightness of the auditorium. In a circle they stood at the heart of the great pulsing arena like a herd of animals, unconsciously awaiting a pronouncement from the gods.

The crowd was restless and expectant. Another announcement carved into the air. '21 Glidiots tonight. Total I.Q. - 630.'

The crowd erupted into rapturous glee. 'And we thought we were dumb!' yelled out someone from the lower tier. This further delighted the crowd.

'It's their own fault!' said Miriam to her brother. 'I'm never going to gamble!'

'Good,' chipped in her mother.

Ushers led the Glidiots by leashes towards the outsides of the arena. Each was given a small gun. Each looked dumbly from gun to usher with the heavy eyes of the truly stupid.

The ushers departed. Steel doors snapped shut to become part of an unbroken steel wall encircling the empty centre of the playing field.

A hush came over the crowd.

Twenty-one Glidiots, their collars flashing, their eyes dull, looked from guns to one another, each seemingly unaware of what was to come. The large muscular man, who looked to be the most alert of the bunch, seemed to have a dim memory of instructions recently given, but long forgotten.

'He'll work it out first,' Marcus whispered.

A loud siren sounded. The crowd percolated into life. The lower level roared in one burst of communal adrenalin. Those in the dress circle remained seated but cheered mightily, and none more mightily than Marcus and Miriam, who loved The Games.

'I sometimes wish I was on the lower tier!' Miriam screamed to Marcus. 'They always seem to have more fun!'

'As long as you're not looking for conversation!' Marcus screamed back.

Horizontal sections in the floor of the central playing area slid back. From these horizontal slits, vertical metal slats sprang up, each connecting to one another in various formations. An instant maze.

Around its edge the twenty-one Glidiots stood, blinking. The crowd yelped and whooped. For some time, the Glidiots did nothing. The crowd's pleasure increased and laughter erupted.

'It won't be long now,' commented Joseph, nodding towards the big man.

Sure enough, the big man began to inspect his weapon closely. He looked straight down its barrel.

'Don't shoot yourself,' Josephine closed one eye as she watched the large Glidiot peer into the loaded gun's interior.

A loud gunshot reverberated through the arena. Silence for a moment.

An announcement boomed out. 'Contestant 16 has blown his head off!'

The crowd roared. The noise from the lower tier was voluminous. Unlike the upper tier, they did not enjoy the safety of protective glass and so their joy resounded unabated through the dome.

'A few wasted I.Q. points, but not many,' resumed the commentary.

More laughter from the masses.

'Twenty Glidiots remain.'

His dog collar no longer flashing, the small man who had just shot himself in the forehead, was dragged out through a chasm which suddenly appeared in the wall, and then closed up just as suddenly. A smear of blood was his only epitaph, but he would still be of use.

The big man was still standing. He looked at his gun, to the crowd, then back again. An idea seemed to be forming in his mind.

One or two of the other contestants also looked perplexed and from gun to crowd, but it was the big man who acted first. He began to walk around the outside of the maze.

'I told you,' Joseph commented and settled back smugly into his seat as he watched the big Glidiot's ape-like march clockwise around the edge of the maze.

The large Glidiot first encountered a tall, thin man, of perhaps twenty. The man appeared completely unaware of what was to come, for he simply stood stationary, his arm hanging limply beside him, as if the weight of the gun was more of a nuisance than his potential salvation.

The thin man stared at the big man. The big man raised his gun and pointed it at the thin man. The thin man continued to stare. He almost smiled, as if to make friends. The crowd hushed. The big man began to squeeze the trigger. The thin man still stared. The crowd was silent. The big man pulled the trigger. The thin man no longer stared. The crowd was no longer silent.

The image of several young members of the crowd burst onto a screen above the maze. There they were, their arms raised in triumph, splattered in blood for all the civilized world to see. This game was being televised throughout Corporate City.

'He's just earned himself 10 I.Q. points,' rattled out the announcer, and the crowd cheered.

The thin man's body was removed and the big man moved on. He came upon an old man and shot him in the head. Another 10 points.

With two more kills the big man's countenance changed. He became more self-assured, stealthier in his gait and purposeful in his demeanour.

But then, another gun shot from another part of the arena, and then another and another.

'Someone else has got the idea,' said Marcus pointing to a rather fat young man who also walked around the extremity of the maze annihilating all in his path.

'I still think the big one will win!' Miriam yelled over the enthusiastic crowd.

'Put some points on him, Dad!' yelled Marcus, gesturing to a keypad mounted into the seat in front of his father.

'We don't gamble, son. You know that!' Joseph yelled back over the noise of the boisterous crowd. Marcus pouted and went back to his cheering.

A sudden realisation hit the crowd. The two men

were about to meet. No other contestants stood between them. The other dozen Glidiots were still motionless, swaying gently from side to side on the far side of the arena.

Total silence.

The big man saw the fat man. He raised his gun. The fat man did not stare. The fat man did not stand still. The fat man jumped sideways into the protection of the maze. The big man froze in alarm.

High above, President Viles laughed to see the first rat in the maze. As he did so, he quietly slid his hand between the legs of his girlfriend. Her eyes widened and she drew in her breath slightly.

Having forced the fat man into the maze, the big man seemed to have another idea. He turned and retraced his steps walking anti-clockwise, until he reached the other unsuspecting Glidiots.

This proved to be a good strategy. He managed to terminate nine more before the fat man emerged from the maze, like a lower order consumer, to claim the final three and then disappear into the maze just as quickly.

The announcer's voice boomed: 'The score is 12 to 6. Contestant 13 has the advantage. He has added 120 I.Q. points. Contestant 8 has added only 60.'

'The cruel thing is that now they both understand what's at stake,' said Miriam with a tinge of pity.

The fat man was encumbered by his overindulged body and was floundering around the maze, knocking into walls, and generally making his whereabouts known to the big man. He was sweating, panicking - a hunted rabbit lost in a labyrinth.

The unforgiving crowd laughed and jeered and watched to see what the big man would do. He was now smarter than anyone in the bottom tier and they knew it. While some still had the confidence to catcall, most were silenced by the tension. He had his prey at hand. What would he do?

What he did was unexpected. He put down his gun. This silenced even the catcallers.

He said, 'I don't wish to kill you. You can come out.'

The crowd began jeering loudly - encouraging the kill.

The fat man cautiously emerged from the maze, holding his gun before him. Comically, he poked his head around the corner of a wall, saw the big man, withdrew, and then repeated the action. He could see that his opponent was unarmed, but he could not command his fear enough to leave the maze. Some in the crowd found this hilarious; others had points on the fat man and were not so amused.

'Kill him! Kill him!' the cry arose from the restless mass.

'This is a first,' Joseph said aloud, sitting forward in his seat.

The fat man quivered with fear while the president said something into a handset, and in one tremendous downward whoosh, the entire maze withdrew leaving the two men out in the open - face to face. Once again, the crowd shut up.

'I don't want to kill you,' repeated the big man. 'Let's not fight.' And he held out his hand.

The silence was thick upon the fat man. Nervously, he licked his lips. At around I.Q. 90, (the 30 he started with and the 60 he had murderously earned), he was on par with the lower tier. They related to him. They watched him intently and he looked at them for a clue, but there was no advice forthcoming. He was a sweaty fat man alone in a huge arena - twenty thousand through the gates, over a million watching at home.

After an eternity of seconds, he made his move. He took aim at the big man. This proved to be a poor decision. Before he could execute the shot, the big man rolled forward with some unknown expertise and in one motion, regained his gun and fired. He hit the fat man in the chest just as the fat man discharged his weapon. The bullet ripped past the big man and into the crowd. An I.Q. 62 never knew what hit her and the crowd erupted.

There was sorrow in the big man's eyes and he sighed and bowed his head as the walls opened and a cavalcade of pageantry burst forth to crown him unwilling 'King for a Night'.

Marcus and Miriam watched the strange expression upon their father's face. Though he should have been elated, he was not.

'Are you alright, Dad?' asked Miriam.

But Joseph did not answer.

'Joseph?' added Josephine, lightly touching his arm.

'Yes. I'm fine,' he whispered.

The big man was being paraded on a float around the outside of the arena - garlands hung askew upon his head, lost in the chaos of his black hair. He was a fitting victor: that handsome face, that manly square jaw and now those intelligent blue eyes. The doleful king regarded the crowd with newfound intelligence.

He passed the position where Joseph and his family were seated. Almost involuntarily, Joseph stood up. This was not protocol for the upper tiers and several people around him protested by pointing out the rude man to their children.

'That is how they behave in the lower tier,' one woman was admonishing her son and casting a disapproving eye towards Josephine, evidently the cause of it because she was his wife.

'Joseph,' protested Josephine, embarrassed, 'please sit down.'

But Joseph was unmoved by pleas to behave appropriately. He caught the eye of the big man and the two exchanged - what was it? A connection? An idea? Something.

In that noisy moment, a silent pact was formed. The big man's float moved past and Joseph sat.

'What was that about?' asked Miriam, wide-eyed at her father's unusual lack of decorum.

Joseph bit his lip in thought, and still oblivious to the 'tut-tuts' of disapproval still intermittently springing around him, he said, 'Let's go and meet him.'

With that, he left. His family looked quizzically, one to the other, then gathered their things and followed.

Far above, as the buzzing crowd exited that giant fishbowl, the president's helicopter was already taking off.

Mark lives in Bowen Mountain, Sydney Australia. He has a wife, Jo-Anne, and two children, Elliot and Imogen.

He writes novels, plays and songs. This novel is the second in The DNA Trilogy and part of a six-part series, the second trilogy of which is titled: The I.Q. Trilogy. All these novels will be released in the near future.

He has taught English and Drama in NSW public high schools for 42 years and now he has finished teaching he is giving more attention to his creative endeavours. He has podcasts and lots of other songs and writings at: markclark.com.au

He has narrated all of his novels and these audiobooks will be available as the books are released.